EX

To Lindy's surprise, nival building swung op against it. She peered insi There, before her very eyes, stood the carnival carousel.

Her heart racing, Lindy tiptoed around the carousel, counting the animals—two abreast, twenty-four in all. No two were alike: the lion with his proud mane, the fierce tiger, the barebacked horse with his front leg raised in a dainty canter—she couldn't decide which one was the most wonderful. Where on earth could all these splendid animals have come from?

No one else knew about the carousel, and Lindy wouldn't tell anyone, either. It was her secret—hers and hers alone. . . .

From THE SECRET CAROUSEL
by Claudia Mills

"Mills's picture of a young girl trying to figure out important decisions for herself is carefully drawn . . . unexpectedly resonant."   —*Booklist*

"A pleasant, warm book which clearly expresses the truth that individuals are free to choose what they are to make out of their lives."   —*School Library Journal*

Other Bantam-Skylark Books you might enjoy
Ask your bookseller for the books you have missed

BOARDWALK WITH HOTEL by Claudia Mills
BELLA ARABELLA by Liza Fosburgh
TOP SECRET by John Reynolds Gardiner
SEBASTIAN (SUPER SLEUTH) AND THE HAIR OF THE
    DOG MYSTERY by Mary B. Christian
BEST FRIENDS (Sweet Valley Twins #1) created by
    Francine Pascal
WHO WANTS A TURNIP FOR PRESIDENT, ANYWAY? by
    Laurie Adams and Allison Coudert
YOUR FORMER FRIEND, MATTHEW by Lou Ann Gaeddert
THE OWLSTONE CROWN by X. J. Kennedy
NUTTY FOR PRESIDENT by Dean Hughes
THE COMEBACK DOG by Jane Resh Thomas
ANNE OF GREEN GABLES by L. M. Montgomery

THE
SECRET
CAROUSEL

Claudia Mills

A BANTAM SKYLARK BOOK®
TORONTO · NEW YORK · LONDON · SYDNEY · AUCKLAND

RL5, 008-011

*This low-priced Bantam Book
has been completely reset in a type face
designed for easy reading, and was printed
from new plates. It contains the complete
text of the original hard-cover edition.*

NOT ONE WORD HAS BEEN OMITTED.

THE SECRET CAROUSEL

A Bantam Book / published by arrangement with Four Winds Press

PRINTING HISTORY
Four Winds edition published April 1983
Bantam Skylark edition / March 1987
*Skylark Books is a registered trademark of Bantam Books, Inc.
Registered in U.S. Patent and Trademark Office and elsewhere.*

ISBN 0-553-15499-0

Published simultaneously in the United States and Canada

PRINTED IN THE UNITED STATES OF AMERICA

O   0 9 8 7 6 5 4 3 2 1

To Sarah

ONE

"Have you seen him yet?" Gram called out. Lindy pretended not to hear. It was the third time Gram had asked that morning.

Pops, stationed at the front bay window, shook his head. "Not a sign of him." He walked slowly over to the door and looked out through the wire mesh. "Nope," he said.

"It's past eleven. He's usually here by now." Gram emerged from the kitchen, wiping her floury hands on the faded calico apron tied around her stout middle. She took a long look from the window, then joined Pops at the door. "I don't understand why he should be late today."

"Now, Mother, I don't know that he's so late."

"It's getting on to quarter past."

"Maybe the Mitchells invited him in for a drink of water. It's ninety in the shade this morning."

"Well, let me know if you see him." Gram returned to the kitchen to check on her biscuits. Gram wasn't really so anxious about the mail. She just liked to keep Pops company as he waited.

"What do you think, Lindy?" Pops asked. "You think he stopped off at the Mitchells'?"

"I don't know." Lindy blew upward to raise her damp bangs from her sticky forehead. It was too hot to care about the mail. Besides, she never got any mail, anyway.

"Why don't you run down to the road and take a look? You can see a spot farther with your young eyes than we old folks can."

"Okay." It couldn't be that much hotter outdoors than in.

But once she had shut the screen door behind her, Lindy changed her mind. The glaring white heat of the sun struck her full in the face, the brightness of it draining all color from the brown grass and making her squint. It was hot, all right.

One lone tree stood by the side of the road, and Lindy plopped down in the shrinking circle of its shade. The stiff, dry grass prickled under her bare legs. The mailman was nowhere in sight.

Pops waited for the mail like this every Saturday morning. On Sunday, the mailman went to church, like everyone else Lindy knew, and there was no mail delivery. On weekdays, Pops still worked down at Necker Brothers, the tractor company where he had worked for forty years. But in another month he would retire, and then he would spend every morning waiting for the mail. Every morning for the rest of his life.

The mournfulness of the thought caught Lindy short. It wasn't fair to think of her grandfather in such a depressing way. After all, there were lots of things that Lindy herself was going to do every day for the rest of her life, like eating breakfast and getting dressed and brushing her teeth. She had just turned ten, and if she lived to be a hundred she would brush her teeth every day for ninety more years. Twice a day times ninety years times three hundred sixty-five days in a year was—Lindy needed pencil and paper for that multiplication. But at least she would do other things besides brushing her teeth, so that every day would be different. Pops would just wait for the mail.

And Gram and Pops didn't even get very much mail. It would have been different if every day the mailman brought them a thick pile of letters and magazines filled with glossy colored pictures. But they just got gas and electric bills, and the church bulletin, and dull advertising circulars printed on cheap pulp paper. Lindy's older sister, Joan, was the only one who got real mail. Joan was fifteen, and she got fat letters from all the friends she had met at ballet camp earlier in the summer. She was the best dancer in the county, maybe in all of Iowa.

Joan had sent Lindy two letters from camp, addressed just to her, to Miss Linda Webster. Lindy had received only one other letter in her life so far, not counting Christmas and birthday cards. It was from the Champ dog food company. Pops had helped her write a letter of complaint after she found a nail in Shep's supper. Champ's customer service department had sent her coupons to get free dog food, but she never used them. If Champ dog food had nails in it, what did it matter if it was free or not? Lindy had saved all three letters, though.

Joan's letters had been the only good thing about the summer, as far as Lindy was concerned. The rest of it was hot and dry and boring and lonely. The four weeks Joan was away at camp had seemed like four long, empty years.

It was hard living all by herself with Gram and Pops, with Joan far away.

The two sisters had gone to live with their father's parents six years ago, after their mother and father were killed in an automobile accident. They had never been especially close—like friends—but that was because Joan was so much older, and so involved with her ballet. Still, except for the weeks Joan had spent at camp, they had never been apart.

Lindy could hardly remember her parents, but Joan, who was nine when they died, remembered them much better. It was Joan who had told Lindy that their mother had always wanted to be a dancer. Now Joan would be a dancer instead. She always filled the house with the music of the ballet records she practiced to. It had been terribly quiet when she was away.

"Do you see him coming?" It was Pops, calling from the front porch.

"Not yet, Pops. I'm watching."

"Maybe we missed him." Lindy heard the click of the mailbox as Pops checked once again.

Lindy peered down the road toward the Mitchells' weather-beaten farmhouse. The heat lay shimmering over the asphalt, and she could smell patches of fresh, oozing tar.

"Wait a minute, I think I see him!" Over the hill, past the Mitchells', appeared first the mailman's blue cap and then the mailman himself, astride his old bicycle, his sack slung over his shoulder. "He's coming up the hill!"

Pleased with having good news, Lindy turned and darted back into the house. She felt shy if the mailman saw her waiting for him. He didn't have to know that she and Pops had nothing better to do than wait.

Joan was in the middle of setting the table when Lindy came into the kitchen. Her long, light hair was pinned up on top of her head in a neat dancer's bun, and her pink leotard was dark with perspiration. It was a beastly day for practicing, but Joan never let anything interfere with her exercises.

"I'll finish that," Lindy offered. "You look so hot."

"I'm almost done. There!" Joan put down the last knife and fork. Then she placed both hands on the table edge, leaning gently over it as she raised a leg straight behind her in a high arabesque.

"He's here!" Pops sang out from the living room.

Gram looked up from slicing tomatoes. "Bring it on in, Dad. We're all waiting."

"Two circulars, the phone bill, and a letter for Joan." Pops tossed Joan's letter into her lap and gave the phone bill to Gram. Then he handed one circular to Lindy, keeping the other for himself. "Grove Hardware's having a sale, I guess," he said, thumbing through the advertisement. "I might go down and get some fertilizer." But Lindy knew he probably wouldn't go.

She laid her circular aside without looking at it. She knew there would never be any mail for her, but every day she was disappointed when there wasn't. Maybe, when school started, Mrs. Adams would have the fifth grade send away for pen pals. That's what she did when Joan was in fifth grade.

"What is it, honey? Bad news?" Pops asked. Lindy looked over at Joan, who sat holding her letter with a strange expression on her face.

"Good news, I guess. It's from Aunt Bea. She came to see our final ballet at camp. You remember." Aunt Bea was their mother's sister and their only relative on that side of the family, except for Grandma Neilson, who lived in Florida. Aunt Bea was a great supporter of all the arts, but she loved ballet best. It had meant a lot to Joan when Aunt Bea had come to watch her dance.

Joan hesitated for a minute, looking hard at Gram and Pops. "Well, she wants me to come stay with her in New York. She says she's willing to pay for my schooling and all my lessons. She's already talked to one of the teachers at the School of American Ballet about me. It's the best school there is."

No one said anything. Then Pops forced a big smile: "It sounds like a wonderful opportunity, if you ask me," he said. "Your Aunt Bea is mighty generous."

Gram placed the big bowl of macaroni salad next to the plate of deviled eggs in the middle of the table and motioned to Lindy to begin serving herself. Lindy just sat there.

"But—well, should I go?" Joan asked. "Can I go?"

"I don't know that we have to decide anything today, do we, Mother?" Pops said, patting Joan's hand, which still held fast to the letter.

"That's right. Now eat up, all of you. There's plenty more in the refrigerator. Take some salad, Lindy, and pass it to your sister."

"I'm not very hungry," Lindy said. She knew Gram and Pops wouldn't stand in the way of her sister's dream. The four dull, lonely weeks of Joan's ballet camp suddenly stretched ahead into months and months, maybe years. Maybe even forever.

"No one's hungry in this heat," Gram said, "but the good Lord meant us to eat, all the same."

TWO

The corn in August was higher than the top of Lindy's head when she stretched up to her toes. It was taller than Pops, who stood six feet tall without his shoes on. It was tall and thickly planted, and there was more of it in Iowa than in any other state in the Union. Some years Illinois had the better crop, but this year all the papers said the prize would go to Iowa again.

Lindy sometimes chanted encouragement as she trudged the two miles into town. Cornfields lined the North Post Road into Three Churches, and Lindy would singsong as she walked along: "Grow, grow, grow your corn. Grow it nice and tall. Better far than Illinois. Better than them all." The tune was "Row, Row, Row Your Boat," but Lindy had made up the words herself.

Today, though, Lindy wasn't singing to the Mitchells' or Swensons' cornfields. She walked fast, ignoring the small, white butterflies that fluttered in the narrow strip of tall grass between the corn and the road. The hotter she felt, the faster she walked. It was ninety-eight degrees out, but Lindy felt even hotter inside.

It was just as hot in town. Lindy didn't linger in the shade of any of the three churches: Lutheran, Roman Catholic, or her own Presbyterian, with its stained-glass scenes of Moses in the bulrushes and Adam naming the animals. On other days she would have stopped for a Slurpy pop in the grocery store or rested on the swings behind the elementary school. But today she just kept on walking at the same furious pace, right through the center of town and out the other side.

On the road that led south from town, Lindy hurried past the Necker Brothers' tractor lot—where Pops worked—and Bowker's feed silos. The animal feed smelled strongly in the oppressive heat, like a steaming compost pile. But Lindy was used to the smell and hardly noticed it. Past Bowker's was another stretch of cornfield, and then, finally, the old overgrown fairgrounds.

Lindy cut across the ragged grass of the fairgrounds, thick with daisies and blue bachelor's buttons. She had never come this far before on any of her walks, though she had driven by many times with Gram and Pops. Beyond lay only endless cornfields, and then more cornfields, all the way to Middleton, six miles farther south. There was no point in walking anymore, even if her feet had not begun to throb from pounding along the scorching asphalt. Exhausted, Lindy headed for a clump of poplar trees and threw herself on the ground beneath them.

If she told Joan how she felt, would Joan refuse to go? If she explained to her about the terrible boredom and loneliness of those four weeks in July, would Joan politely decline Aunt Bea's invitation? Lindy didn't know, and the awful thing was that she wasn't even certain which answer she would really want Joan to give. If Joan passed up Aunt Bea's offer, Lindy would know that her request had prevented Joan from becoming the best dancer she could possibly be. Lindy wanted Joan to be the prima ballerina of the world. She ached with pride whenever she watched her sister dance.

Unless—unless Joan wrote to Aunt Bea and asked if Lindy could come, too! Lindy sprang up in sudden excitement. Aunt Bea had lots of money—she was a lawyer with one of the fanciest firms in New York City. Two sisters couldn't be much more expensive than one. And Lindy would make sure that she hardly cost anything. She would work hard around the apartment and make herself useful in so many ways that she would be earning her keep in no time at all. She wouldn't ask for special lessons or new clothes or anything. All she wanted was not to be left behind when Joan went away.

Gram and Pops would be sure to let her go, if they gave their permission to Joan. They had always been scrupulously fair. They would be bound to miss her some, of course, since she was home so much more than Joan, who took dance classes six times a week and went out on the weekend with friends from the regional high. Lindy's school bus brought her home at three o'clock every day, and even though she sometimes had homework, she would spend hours stitching together squares for Gram's quilts or playing cribbage with Pops.

Pops had told her one evening while Joan was off at camp that he didn't know what he'd do to pass the time if Lindy wasn't there. Gram never said anything like that, but Gram would miss her, too. Not that they wouldn't let her go. Lindy knew that Gram and Pops loved her very much and that they would sacrifice anything for her happiness.

Slowly, Lindy dropped back down on the hard dirt. She couldn't go to New York with Joan. Joan could go because she had to, as a dancer. If you had a gift like Joan's, it would be wrong to hide it under a bushel. Joan had to set her gift high on the mountaintops so that it would shine like a beacon all over the world. That was what it said in the Bible. But Lindy didn't have any special gift that shouldn't be hidden away in Three Churches, Iowa. And she would hurt Gram and Pops so much if she asked to go away. She couldn't leave Pops behind all alone to wait for the mail without her. No, Joan would go, and Lindy would stay.

Lindy pulled out one long blade of grass and nibbled meditatively at its tender, pale root. She didn't feel happy about her decision, but she felt right about it. She felt like a good person, and that was supposed to be better than feeling happy. Rolling over onto her stomach, she watched a ladybug make its way up her brown arm. The ladybug wasn't afraid of her. It probably knew that this arm belonged to somebody kind and good.

The fairgrounds were deserted today as they always were, at least as long as Lindy could remember. Ages ago there had been an enormous carnival here at the end of every summer, Pops had told them. Farmers and their families had come from miles around, and from sunrise until midnight the dusty fields had been trampled by noisy crowds of merrymakers. The agricultural exhibits had been the finest in the state, with prizes given for everything from the fattest hogs to the longest ears of corn. Lindy's great-grandfather had taken the grand prize for pumpkins once, and Gram's quilts had come away with blue ribbons two years in a row.

Lindy loved when Pops told them about the strolling clowns who would turn cartwheels and juggle Indian clubs, and the mysterious gypsy fortune-tellers who would look into your future if you crossed their palms with silver. One old woman had said that Gram would marry a tall, dark stranger who lived across the ocean, so everything they said didn't always come true. But it would be thrilling to have your fortune told, all the same.

There had been rides, too. Pops's favorite story was about the tall Ferris wheel, and how it had gotten stuck one windy night just as Pops was trapped at the very top! Lindy shivered at the thought. But best of all had been the carousel, where splendid circus animals had pranced in time to the calliope.

Pops took on a special glow when he talked about the carousel. Every animal was different, he said, and you had your choice of a lion, a tiger, a zebra, a bear—any animal you could think of. It was like having a whole zoo come to town.

But all that had been years and years ago, back when Pops and Gram were courting. Now folks who wanted a good time drove off to the city or waited for the big state fair. All that was left of the old carnival days was a few unpainted wooden buildings set back from the road. It made Lindy sad to think of all the holiday crowds that didn't come to the fairgrounds any longer.

Since she had come all this way, Lindy figured that she might as well explore a little bit. No one would mind if she poked into the old carnival buildings—it had been so long since anybody took an interest in those weather-beaten gray shacks. She brushed the ladybug gently from her elbow and stood up, rubbing the red grass marks crisscrossed on the back of her legs.

There were three buildings on the fairgrounds: two small sheds and a larger barnlike structure. Lindy limped over to the first small shed—the long, hot walk in her stiff-backed new sneakers had given her a raw blister on her left heel. She found a tiny window that she could reach if she stood on tiptoe, but she couldn't see anything in the shadowy darkness within. She pushed hard against the door. The rusty old hinges didn't budge. Disappointed, she tried the second shed, but it was locked as well, and all she could make out through the sooty windowpane was some old farm implements leaning against the far wall.

All the windows on the big building were higher than eye level. But, to Lindy's surprise, the sturdy door swung open slowly when she pushed against it. She peered inside, wondering if she would see anything more exciting than ancient farm equipment, and gasped in astonishment. There, before her very eyes, stood the carnival carousel.

It was the same carousel, just as Pops had described it so many times, abandoned now in this forgotten barn. Lindy had taken for granted that it had disappeared with the brightly lit Ferris wheel and the wandering gypsies. No one in Three Churches seemed to know or care that it was still here, where it had always been. Certainly Pops had never mentioned it.

Her heart racing, Lindy tiptoed around the carousel, counting the animals—two abreast, twenty-four in all. Sure enough, no two were alike. The lion with his proud mane, the fierce tiger, the barebacked horse with his front leg raised in a dainty canter—she couldn't decide which one was most wonderful. The camel, maybe, with his funny hump, or the performing seal, twirling a striped beach ball on the tip of his nose. Where on earth could all these splendid animals have come from?

Their paint was faded, chipped, and peeling now. Hardly one was without an injury; the giraffe's neck was cracked almost in two. Lindy felt a lump of love rise up in her throat for all of them, these old, faithful wooden animals, waiting tirelessly for a new crowd of laughing children. She reached over and stroked the seal's dusty nose.

No one else knew about the carousel, and Lindy wouldn't tell anyone, either, not Gram or Joan, not even Pops. It was her secret, and that was how it would stay— hers and hers alone.

THREE

Lindy sprawled across her bed, watching her sister pack. Joan's bed was piled high with neatly folded underwear, blouses, sweaters, jeans, skirts, all labeled with Joan's name. Gram had made them sew a tag in every single item, just as if Joan were going back to camp. Joan had done her share of grumbling about the sewing, but she looked happy now, as she bustled back and forth from one pile to another.

"Hey, Shep!" Lindy said softly, and the old collie, lying beneath her bed, beat his tail feebly on the rug. He was twelve years old, and since one person-year equaled seven dog-years, that meant he was eighty-four years old, older even than Gram or Pops.

"Don't get him all worked up," Joan said, depositing a stack of underwear in her trunk. "He's so old."

"He likes it," Lindy said. "Don't you, Shep? Huh, Shep?" The thumping became more vigorous, and Shep gave a faint, yelping bark. "You're going to sleep in Joan's bed when she's gone, right, Shep?"

"Oh, Lindy, even you couldn't stand that more than one night, not the way he smells."

"He doesn't smell so bad."

"He sure does."

Shep padded out from under the bed, and Joan stooped down to give him a kiss. "Ugh," she said. "You stink, Shep."

Joan had a separate suitcase set aside for her ballet things, and she began slowly pulling rainbow-colored tights and leotards from her middle bureau drawer.

"What if it turns out that I'm no good?" she asked suddenly, when the suitcase was halfway full.

"What are you talking about?"

"What if I fail at my audition for the school, and they send me away?"

"They won't."

"How do you know they won't?"

"They just won't." If Lindy was sure of anything, it was that Joan was going to be the greatest ballerina in the world. "Aunt Bea has probably seen a million ballets, and *she* thought you were wonderful."

"But there are so many things only a dancer can see."

"*Anybody* can see that you're the best dancer there is," Lindy insisted. "Anybody with eyes, that is."

"Oh, Lindy, I'm going to miss you," Joan said, coming to sit beside her, ballet slipper in hand. "I really am."

"I'm going to miss you, too," Lindy said. She didn't add that she was probably going to miss Joan a thousand times more than Joan would miss her.

"So how many days till school starts?"

Lindy shrugged. "I don't know. Next week, I think." This year she hadn't even bothered to count. She would just be riding on the same bus with the same kids to the same school where the same teacher had taught fifth grade for twenty years.

"Have you picked a foreign country yet, for your yearlong independent project?" Joan asked. Mrs. Adams even assigned the same projects year after year.

"No," Lindy said, trying not to sound as cross as she suddenly felt. "Which one did you do?"

La belle France." Joan gestured grandly with her ballet slipper. "I'd love to dance there when I'm in a company. Maybe we'll tour throughout Europe."

New York, France, all of Europe—Lindy felt more and more miserable. She hopped up from the bed and threw her arms around Shep. He wasn't going to abandon her for the wide world.

"You'll take care of Gram and Pops, won't you?" Joan asked then, and something in her voice made Lindy look back up at her.

"You know I will."

"You think they'll be okay?"

"I guess so." Joan still looked worried, and Lindy forced herself to sound more cheerful. "I mean, of course they'll be okay."

It was an hour's drive to the airport in Des Moines, but Gram and Pops had them leave the house at two-thirty for a five-thirty flight. There might be traffic, Pops said.

"Now, what are you going to do if Bea isn't there when you get off the plane?" Gram asked over her shoulder, as Pops drove along ten miles under the speed limit, the way he always did.

"Ask a flight attendant to have her paged," Joan recited glibly.

"And if she doesn't come then?"

"Call her apartment, notify a policeman, and wait right where I am. But she'll be there, Gram."

"Don't forget to call us as soon as your trunk arrives," Pops added.

"I won't." Joan's huge old trunk was being shipped separately to New York, so she had only two suitcases to carry with her on the flight. One was the ballet suitcase, of course.

Six cars in a row had passed Pops's ancient Chevrolet. Lindy had counted them. She wished he would drive a little faster. "Are we going to be late?" she asked.

"Nope," Pops said. "Plenty of time. Leave earlier, drive slower, live longer. That's what I always say."

The seventh car whizzed by on the left. "Everyone's in such a big hurry," Pops said. "I find myself wondering: Where are they all going that's so almighty important they're willing to risk their necks to get there two minutes sooner?"

Lindy sighed and tried not to squirm with impatience. Joan gave her a sympathetic smile. Lindy knew Joan had reason to be twice as impatient. Joan was going to fly on a real airplane for the very first time. In a few hours, she would be able to peer down out of the plane window and see Three Churches looking like a toy railroad town, and Pops's big Chevy creeping along home like a tiny ladybug on a thin black ribbon. And then she would land in New York, and every day there would be something new and exciting.

"They'll probably give you supper on the plane," Gram said, "but you just tell them that you aren't supposed to have any. You've never flown before, and you don't know how your stomach is going to like it."

"I'm sure I'll feel just fine," Joan said. Gram gave her a wise, pitying look. "But I won't have any supper, I promise." She crossed her fingers behind her back for Lindy's benefit, and Lindy stifled a giggle.

The airport wasn't very crowded, and they all waited in line with Joan to check her luggage and get her boarding pass.

"Tell the man you want an aisle seat," Gram whispered when Joan's turn was next. "It'll be easier if you need to use the restroom."

"Smoking or nonsmoking?" the red-jacketed man behind the counter asked. He gave Joan a special smile. *Maybe he saw her class perform in Des Moines last spring,* Lindy thought. *Maybe he knows she's going off to New York to become a famous dancer.*

"Nonsmoking."

"Aisle or window?"

"Window, please." Joan darted a mischievous glance at Gram and then gave her a quick hug. "I'll be okay, Gram. Really, I will."

Everyone managed to keep a cheerful appearance until, finally, the flight was announced and Joan was ready to board. Then Gram dabbed at her eyes with a hanky, and Lindy worked to blink back tears. Pops smiled down at Joan extra hard, and it looked to Lindy as if Joan might cry, except that her sister never cried. Joan gave them each a last hug, and then turned and walked through the gate without looking back.

In the car on the slow ride home, Pops asked Lindy gruffly, "So you think that sister of yours will be all right?"

"I'm sure she will," Lindy said. Two more cars sped by Pops, honking loudly. Lindy had promised Joan that Gram and Pops would be fine, and now she had promised Gram and Pops that Joan would be fine. But who was going to make sure that Lindy would be all right?

FOUR

School started the week after Joan left, and Lindy watched the day draw closer with steadfast indifference. Other summers she had hung an enormous calendar chart on her closet door and crossed off every day till school began. Lindy's best friends from school, Nan and Alice, both lived on the other side of town, too far for her to see much of them during the summer. None of the neighbors had children even close to her age. So ordinarily school was something to be excited about. But this year Lindy had taken the calendar down after Joan got her letter from Aunt Bea. Why make a big fuss over another school year in Three Churches?

Mrs. Adams had taught fifth grade in Three Churches for twenty years, and every year she taught it exactly the same way. In September, everyone picked a country for their big yearlong project on Nations of the World. Last year, in fourth grade, the big project had been on American geography, and Lindy had picked Vermont. She liked the way the name of the state sounded next to the name of the capital: Vermont, Montpelier. She said it over and over again to herself when she couldn't sleep at night. But this year the project didn't interest Lindy in the slightest. She didn't want to *study* a foreign country—she wanted to *live* in one.

October was the month for fractions, and the student with the highest score on the final fractions test got to bring in the class pumpkin. Joan had taught Lindy lots about fractions already, giving her a pretty good chance of being the best. But Pops didn't grow pumpkins, so the honor would be an empty one. The class pumpkin! Lindy was sure fifth graders in New York would scoff at the very idea.

In November, they sent away for pen pals. That would be a little better, mostly because of Pops. It would be something to see Pops's face when the postman delivered a special airmail letter from a faraway foreign country. Lindy would let them read it, too, so waiting for the mail wouldn't be such a waste of time anymore. And if Lindy ever went to Europe, she would already have a friend waiting for her there. But November was a long time away still. In fact, as far as Lindy was concerned, the two months till November stretched ahead like all of eternity.

Gram had made her a new blue corduroy jumper to wear on the first day. Joan thought blue was a good color for Lindy because it made her eyes look bluer and her hair blonder. Lindy's hair was the color people called dirty blond, not really blond like Joan's, but more blond than brown. Lindy didn't mind the color, but she hated the name. It made it sound as if she didn't wash her hair as often as Joan did. But the blue jumper was pretty, anyway, with a ruffle along the bottom and a bow on the back.

That first morning, Lindy was out of the house fifteen minutes before the bus. Whatever she felt, nothing could be more terrible than to miss the bus on the first day of school. While she waited, she wondered what Joan was doing right that very minute. Maybe Joan was riding off to school on a swift, gleaming subway. Or, she was already in class, high on top of one of the skyscrapers. New York was in a different time zone, so eight o'clock for Lindy was nine o'clock for Joan.

Lindy's bus finally lumbered by. Mr. Townsend, the bus driver, gave Lindy a big wink. Nan and Alice took a different bus to school, so Lindy sat with Meg O'Neill, whose family lived a few miles farther out on the Post Road. Meg had been to the Grand Canyon over the summer, and that made Lindy feel even worse about her long, dull days at home. She couldn't remember if Mrs. Adams made you write what you did during your summer vacation. *I waited for the mail every day. I got two letters.*

She met Nan and Alice outside the fifth-grade door. Nan, who had three brothers, was brown as an acorn from playing outside all summer, and Alice, prettier even than Joan, seemed taller and thinner. She looked more grown-up than the rest of them did, with her hair pulled up off her neck by a flowered barrette. Not that Joan wouldn't look twice as sophisticated, now that she lived in the city.

"I heard your sister went away to New York," Alice said. Her mother must have seen Gram in the grocery store.

"Uh-huh. Last week." She could add to her composition: *I went to the airport. Twenty-seven cars passed us on the way*.

Nan gave her hand a quick little squeeze of sympathy. Lindy squeezed back automatically, but then she pulled her hand away.

"Joan's going to study at the best ballet school in the country," she said. People should be feeling envious of Joan, not sorry for Lindy.

The bell rang loudly, and the fifth graders moved into line. With Alice ahead of her and Nan behind, like every year since kindergarten, Lindy marched into fifth grade.

The classroom looked just as Lindy knew it would. Autumn leaves cut from red, orange, and yellow construction paper lined the narrow strip of bulletin board above the chalkboard. In between the leaves hung patriotic quotations neatly lettered on yellowing oaktag: "Give me liberty or give me death."—Patrick Henry; "I only regret that I have but one life to lose for my country."—Nathan Hale. The side bulletin board was empty, with "Our Summer Vacations" in construction-paper letters across the top. Lindy's heart sank.

She, Nan, and Alice chose seats together halfway back—Lindy and Nan side by side, and Alice right behind. Mrs. Adams might want to assign seats, so Lindy waited to unpack her knapsack. Gram had made sure she had a fat new notebook and lots of pencils and pens, colored ones, too. It would be fun arranging everything in her new desk. As much fun as anything in Three Churches could be, she reminded herself.

After they saluted the flag, Mrs. Adams took attendance, perching her funny half-glasses on her nose to read the list of names. Mrs. Adams was tall and thin, with black hair pulled back in a bun and a mouth that had a friendly way of turning up at the corners in a sudden smile. She stood absolutely straight with her shoulders back, and her voice was strong and clear as she called out the roll.

"Michael Acton."

"Here."

"Anne-Marie Auerbach."

"Here."

Lindy was always the last one to be called. Mickey Acton once said it had been proven scientifically that people whose names begin with the last letters of the alphabet are less successful than people whose names begin with the first. They just have to spend too much time waiting for their turn to be called. Mickey Acton would say that, of course, being an *A*. But Lindy had pointed out that George Washington had been a *W*, and he had turned out all right.

"Linda Webster."

"Here."

Mrs. Adams made the final mark in her roll book. "Are you Joan's sister?" she asked.

Lindy nodded. Teachers always remembered Joan, so she was used to the question. It never bothered her, the way it bothered some kids. She liked to have people know she was related to Joan.

Mrs. Adams smiled. "Now, class," she said, "the first thing I'm going to ask you to do this morning is to write a short composition on how you spent your summer. I'm sure your classmates would like to know what interesting things you've all been doing since last June. And let's make this the year for nice, legible penmanship, shall we?"

She passed out white, lined paper. Lindy stared despairingly down at the blank sheet. Nan's family had gone camping to a lake up in Minnesota. Alice had spent a month at church camp and learned to ride a horse. Standing in line before the bell rang, Lindy had heard a couple of the boys talking about a week-long Boy Scout expedition. Everyone had something to write about except her. She was too boring even for this boring assignment.

What could she find to fill up two paragraphs? Well, Lindy was helping Gram stitch strips together for a "log cabin" quilt. Shep had had his twelfth dog-birthday, and Lindy had had her tenth person-birthday. She had beaten Pops four times in a row at cribbage.

Lindy bit savagely at the new pink eraser on the tip of her sharpest pencil. It wasn't fair that she should have to write about quilts and cribbage and dog birthdays. How could she get points for composition when anything she wrote would be so short and dull? Maybe next summer she would visit Joan in New York, and then she'd write about going all the way up the Empire State Building and seeing the Atlantic Ocean stretch across the globe to England and to Spain. She would write about subways deep under the ground, buried beneath buildings so tall that on cloudy days you couldn't see the tops of them. But in sixth grade they probably didn't have vacation compositions.

Lindy glanced over at Nan's paper. "What I Did This Summer" was printed across the first line. This summer, next summer—it didn't make that much difference, did it? The point of the assignment was just to practice writing, after all. It shouldn't matter whether what you wrote about was in the past or future.

"My Next Summer," Lindy put down, and then, bursting with ideas, she began writing faster and faster, trying to get them all down, all the adventures she would have, all the sights she would see. She finished one side of the page and was about to flip it over when she looked up and saw Mrs. Adams standing by her desk.

"Maybe I wasn't clear," Mrs. Adams said kindly, in a low voice so the others wouldn't hear. "I meant for you to write about what you did *last* summer."

"I didn't do anything," Lindy said, feeling her face grow red.

"Oh, but of course you did. There's plenty for you to write about, even if you stayed right here at home. It doesn't have to be anything exciting. What's important is that it happened to *you*. Now, let me get you a fresh sheet of paper, and you can start again. If you need more time to finish, you can turn this in tomorrow."

Lindy bit her lip to keep from crying. She crumpled "My Next Summer" into a tight ball and stuffed it in the back of her desk.

"My dog Shep had a birthday," she wrote on the clean sheet. "He was twelve."

FIVE

After forty years at Necker Brothers, Friday was going to be Pops's last day. He would walk out the door on Friday afternoon and never go back to work again.

"What will you do instead?" Lindy asked him Friday morning at breakfast. Gram was making griddle cakes, the way she always did on special occasions.

"Whatever I want to do," Pops said.

"Like what?"

"I don't know—take whole days just to go fishing, putter around in the garden, clean up my basement shop. No siree, Lindy, the days aren't going to be long enough for all I've a mind to do."

Lindy thought that over. She didn't think Pops had gone fishing or puttered in the garden once since she had come to Three Churches. And his basement shop was immaculate, without a speck of sawdust anywhere. It had been years since Pops had touched his saw.

"Who will do the books when you're gone?" she asked, to change the subject.

"I reckon they'll find someone. Nobody's irreplaceable, you know. Folks may think they are, but they find out otherwise soon enough." Pops tucked in his large cloth napkin more securely at his collar. He was wearing a jacket and tie so he would look nice for the photographer at the luncheon banquet Necker's was giving in his honor.

"More griddle cakes, Lindy?" Gram asked.

"Uh-huh," Lindy said, her mouth still full from her last bite. "I mean, yes, please."

Gram flipped two more griddle cakes onto Lindy's plate and sat down at the table. "It'll be strange to have a man underfoot all day," she said.

"But nice," Lindy added. She didn't want Pops's feelings to be hurt.

"We'll see," Gram said.

Pops laughed. "I think I can keep out of your way, Mother. Fact, you may have to send Lindy here out looking for me down at the firehouse. I plan to play me a lot of poker now that I'm retired." But Lindy knew Pops didn't care for playing cards.

Pops wiped his mouth and crumpled his napkin into a ball. He looked very handsome in his plaid jacket and bright green tie, with his thinning gray hair slicked back from his high forehead.

"Well, I'm off to be honored," he said.

Gram stood up, too, and kissed him good-bye. Shep gave one hearty yelp and then stretched out under Lindy's chair again. When Pops had gone, Lindy saw that Gram had tears in her eyes.

"He loves that job like a part of himself," she said, "and I don't know what he's going to do without it."

"But he wants to retire," Lindy said.

"It doesn't much matter to Necker Brothers whether you want to retire or not," Gram said. "When you turn seventy, it's out you go."

"Do you think he really minds?" Lindy asked. "He wants to go fishing, he said so."

"People say a lot of things. Now finish up those griddle cakes before you're late for your bus."

When Lindy hopped off the bus at three o'clock, Pops was just driving up in his old car. "Come help me carry in all my loot, honey," he called to her. Gram appeared on the porch. "You, too, Mother."

There were three cartons in the backseat of the car, and Lindy took the smallest one. On top of a stack of papers was a framed photograph of her and Joan, taken right before the accident. She was just four in the picture, a chubby little girl with two dirty-blond pigtails. Joan stood next to her, tall and slim like a dancer, with the young ballerina smile she always gave for the camera. That picture had stood on Pops's desk at Necker Brothers for as long as Lindy could remember.

"Was the banquet nice?" Lindy asked when all the cartons were set down in the living room.

"I guess you could say so. It's kind of embarrassing to have a bunch of folks all speechifying about you."

"What did Joe Necker have to say?" Gram asked. Joe was the senior Necker brother.

Pops looked a little self-conscious. "Nothing much. He did say I was the best bookkeeper he had ever seen in all his years of business."

"I should think he'd have the sense to see that by now," Gram said.

"Bob Necker practically broke down when his turn came, poor fellow. Of course, he and I started there just about the same time—July it was, and hot as Hades. They didn't have air conditioning back then, you know. That back office was just sweltering, and I think the two of us went through half a dozen handkerchiefs every day just mopping away at our foreheads." He chuckled appreciatively. "You earned your money back in those days. I can vouch for that."

He fumbled in his pocket and pulled out a small box. "Everyone chipped in to give me this." In the box was a large, round gold watch. "It's solid, all right," Pops said, laying it in his palm. "Must have cost them a pretty penny. It gives you pause when folks think so much of you."

Lindy rubbed her finger lightly over the scrolled design embossed on the front. "Does it work?" she asked.

"You'd better believe it works," Pops said. "If it doesn't, I'm giving it right back."

"You cleaned out your desk," Gram said, picking up a thick manila folder from the middle box. Lindy could see the folder was full of brittle newspaper clippings from all the times Necker Brothers had made the *Evening Sentinel*.

"The new bookkeeper won't want all my junk," Pops said. "I never was any good at throwing anything away."

"I guess you'll want these up in the attic."

"Seems like the best place for them now." Pops took the picture of Lindy and Joan from the box Lindy had carried and set it on the mantelpiece. "I sure did have the two prettiest girls on my desk," he said, reaching over to rumple Lindy's hair.

"I made chicken casserole tonight," Gram said, "since that's your favorite." She picked up the watch without looking at it and then put it down again.

"You're right there, Mother," Pops said. He nudged one of the cartons with his foot. "When I take these up to the attic I'll have to try to find my old fishing gear. It's up there somewhere, isn't it? Monday morning nine o'clock sharp, I plan to be down by the pond catching us a mess of fish."

Gram turned away abruptly, and Pops caught at her hand.

"Now, don't you fret, Mother," he said. "I'm going to enjoy every minute of my retirement. Aren't I, Lindy?"

He winked at Lindy, and, suddenly afraid she'd cry if she didn't, Lindy winked back.

SIX

The little speckled yellow one was the cutest, Lindy decided, sitting next to Pops the next morning as he sorted through his fishing tackle. Pops had two big metal boxes full of lures: tiny fish cut out of shiny metal, wisps of green feathers, fat rubber worms—all to dangle before near-sighted and hungry fish.

"That one's just for stream fishing, honey," Pops said. "For pond fishing worms are the thing."

"Ugh," Lindy said. "I'd hate to be a fish."

"If you were, you'd like a big fat juicy worm just as much as you like blueberry pie right now."

Lindy doubted it. But even if fish did like fat juicy worms, they wouldn't like fake rubber worms stuck on a sharp hook. She felt sorry for the fish.

The phone rang as she sat staring at the small drawer full of worms.

"Dad! Lindy!" Gram called from the kitchen. "It's Joan!"

Lindy jumped up and hurried to the phone, with Pops right behind her. Joan had called once before, after her trunk arrived, but that had been two weeks ago. She had written a couple of times, but Joan's letters were short and skimpy on news.

"You did?" Lindy heard Gram say. "That's very nice. Are you taking the vitamins I gave you?"

What was very nice? Lindy looked at Gram questioningly, but Gram kept on talking.

"Take them with juice if you don't like the taste," Gram said. "Are you sleeping enough . . . ? I'm glad to hear it. You're still growing, you know. Does Bea make sure you're getting green vegetables?"

Lindy and Pops looked at each other impatiently. Gram's checklist could go on forever. But finally Gram said, "I'll let you say hello to your grandfather now," and handed the receiver over to Pops.

"Hi, honey," Pops said. "Why, that's terrific!" It must have to do with ballet, Lindy thought. The fancy New York school must have accepted Joan as a pupil. "I can't say we're surprised, honey, but we sure are proud."

Pops grinned broadly at Lindy as he gave her the phone.

"Hi, Joan," Lindy said, feeling a little shy. She still wasn't used to talking on the phone long distance. "Congratulations."

"I'm just so relieved," Joan said. "It would have been too humiliating to have come all this way for nothing."

"How's New York?"

"It's okay. But how are Gram and Pops? How are you?"

"We're okay, too." Over the crackly connection Joan hardly sounded like her sister, and with Gram and Pops right there Linda couldn't think of anything else to say.

"So what country did you pick?"

That again. "I haven't decided."

"Well, if you want to get off easy, pick Andorra. It's the smallest country in the world."

"Okay," Lindy said. But she couldn't pass the phone back to Gram, not yet, not after saying only a dozen words. "I miss you," she finally said.

"I miss you, too."

Silently, Lindy gave the phone back and tiptoed out the back door into their small yard, surrounded on all sides by neighbors' cornfields. The sky was gray and the cornfields were green, and they both stretched on until they met at the horizon. Lindy stood there for a long time, watching the corn tassels ripple in the growing wind, until the first raindrop plopped onto the hard dirt by her scuffed sneakers.

Pops stuck his head out the back door. "So what do you think about our Joan? She's something, isn't she?"

Lindy nodded, trying to match Pops's big smile. But she just didn't feel like smiling.

"Doesn't look like I'm going fishing today, I guess," Pops said, squinting at the darkening sky. "But the farmers'll be happy. It's been a dry September. Better come inside now, honey. It's going to come down pretty hard."

The ground was splattered all over now with polka dots of rain. Lindy held out her hand to feel a few more cool, wet drops splash against it and then went inside again.

Andorra was a country high in the mountains between France and Spain. Only 20,550 people lived there, and they made their living tending sheep. Lindy knew because she had looked it up in Pops's big *Columbia Encyclopedia*.

As it turned out, Andorra wasn't the *very* smallest country in the world. Liechtenstein and San Marino were both smaller. But Lindy liked Andorra's name best. She would take Joan's suggestion and pick Andorra as her Nation of the World. Gram and Pops had never heard of Andorra, and Lindy was almost certain Mrs. Adams hadn't heard of it, either. Everyone else would pick a commonplace country like France or Mexico, and Lindy would have a country that even the teacher knew nothing about.

It rained hard all afternoon, and Lindy lay on her bed and thought about Andorra. She thought about her secret carousel, too. She hadn't been back there yet, but she would go tomorrow if the rain stopped.

Lindy's bedroom was under the eaves, and the constant pounding of the rain against the roof made her sleepy. She liked the time right before she fell asleep because she could imagine things best then, half-dreaming and half-awake. She could imagine that the carousel animals had come to life, with magical powers to carry her over land and sea to all the places she had ever learned about in school. They would carry her over mountains and oceans, until she reached Andorra, high in the mountains between France and Spain.

As she drifted off to sleep, she heard the words in a dreamy refrain: *high in the mountains between France and Spain.*

SEVEN

"Which country did you pick?" Meg O'Neill asked Lindy on the bus Monday morning, peering out from nder her yellow hooded rain slicker. It was supposed to keep on raining all week.

"I haven't decided," Lindy lied. "What about you?"

"France," Meg said.

Lindy just smiled.

The very first thing, right after the flag salute, Mrs. Adams went directly to the chalkboard. "When I call your name," she said, "tell me the country you've chosen, and I'll write it up here on the board."

Sure enough, five people, including Meg, picked France. Alice picked Sweden, and Nan picked Spain. There were two Italys, three Russias, and one each for Canada, Mexico, England, Scotland, Japan, and the People's Republic of China.

"Lindy Webster."

Lindy had never been more glad to be called on last. "Andorra," she said, watching Mrs. Adams carefully for signs of bewilderment and confusion.

Nan looked blank, and Alice stared back over her shoulder, puzzled. Mrs. Adams didn't say anything for a moment, and Lindy felt her heart racing.

"Andorra's a very small country, Lindy. Do you really think you can find enough information on it to keep you busy all year?"

"I think so." Actually, Lindy hadn't thought about that at all. There had been only one small paragraph about Andorra in Pops's encyclopedia. Did people write books about countries with only 20,550 people in them? What if June came and went and her report was only three pages long?

"There's no bigger country you'd rather do instead?"

Lindy shook her head stubbornly. Mrs. Adams hadn't said they had to pick a *big* country. So what if her report turned out to be the shortest and the worst in the whole class? She wasn't going to like anything about school this year, anyway.

"I have an idea, then. Why don't you work on several of those tiny countries, say, Luxembourg, Monaco, Liechtenstein, San Marino, *and* Andorra. That way you get to keep the one you want, but you'll have more material for your project."

Lindy stared down at her desk. It was a wonderful idea. Her heart yearned toward all those little countries, waiting for her to learn about them. But she kept on staring down at her pencils, neatly lined up all in a row. She wasn't supposed to let herself like anything about Three Churches at all.

"Okay," she muttered, making sure no one could tell she was pleased. "If that's what you want me to do."

After lunch Mrs. Adams made an announcement so grand that even Lindy had trouble restraining her enthusiasm. There was going to be a class play—three plays, in fact, all during the year—real plays, with costumes and scenery and props and regular actors' makeup. Lindy hadn't known that plays were part of fifth grade. She hadn't remembered Joan telling her that Mrs. Adams had been a drama major in college. It was hard enough to imagine Mrs. Adams as a student, period.

The first play was going to take place in the beginning of November, and it was all about the Pilgrims and Thanksgiving. Five boys and five girls would have parts to speak. The class would spend the rest of the week going over the play in their reading groups so they could decide which parts they wanted to try out for. Then they would have auditions on Monday. Anyone who didn't get a part would help with costumes, props, makeup, and prompting. Prompting meant sitting backstage and whispering lines to any actor who'd forgotten them. Lindy knew she would die if she forgot her lines and had to be prompted.

Mrs. Adams told them briefly about each character. The best part by far, Lindy thought, was Patience, the fat old hag who gets put in the stocks for her constant nagging. Patience was the biggest girl's part, and Lindy could just see herself waddling back and forth onstage with a huge pillow tucked under her clothes. But it wouldn't be a real stage, just the front of their same small classroom. And it wasn't a real play, either. Real plays weren't half an hour long, with people's parents and neighbors making up the audience.

She gave a cross scowl like Patience would give. Scowl-ing came easy to Lindy lately. When she got home she would practice it in front of the mirror.

"Is anything the matter, Lindy?" Mrs. Adams asked.

Lindy made the cross scowl disappear, but she still felt like she was scowling deep inside. Her little countries weren't going to change anything, and the class play wasn't going to change anything, either. They could make her stay in Three Churches, but they couldn't make her think that life in Three Churches was anything wonderful.

"No," she said, and sat unsmiling the rest of the afternoon.

EIGHT

PATIENCE: And who gave you leave, my lad, to lay a finger on one of my prize pies?

JOHN: Why, no one. I merely thought—

PATIENCE: *(cuffing him soundly on the ear)* You merely thought, did you? Well, see that next time you think something different!

Lindy slid off the couch to practice cuffs on Shep, who lay uncomplaining as imaginary blows rained about his ears. "'You merely thought, did you?'" she said under her breath, but it didn't sound fierce enough. "'You merely thought, did you?!!'"

"What's that, honey?" Pops asked. The Saturday mail had come hours ago, but Pops sat looking out the window, anyway, watching occasional cars and trucks go by.

"Nothing," Lindy said.

"Is it a play for school?"

"No." Lindy felt bad for lying. "I mean, yes, but I don't want to be in it."

"Why not? Sounds to me like it might be kind of fun." A pickup truck rattled by, and Pops stood up to look.

"I just don't want to." She rummaged through the rug for the needle she had dropped. Gram's big log cabin quilt had 240 squares in it, and each square had 17 strips to stitch. It seemed like the more Lindy sewed, the more there was to sew. The dining room table was covered with fabric, and Gram had been cutting out strips all afternoon. Lindy had opened the play only because she was sick and tired of sewing.

"What's the play about?"

"The Pilgrims. It's for Thanksgiving." She gave up on the needle. She'd have to wait till someone stepped on it.

Pops came over to the couch and picked up the script. "Who's Patience?"

"That's the best part. She's cross and mean and scowls all the time."

"Who's John?"

"He's Ann's brother. And Ann's the one who's in love with the Captain."

Since she had started, she might as well go on and tell Pops the whole story of the play. She knew half the parts by heart, since they had read the play out loud every day in reading group. As she told the story she acted it out, using a deep, hearty, seafaring voice for the Captain and a sweet, lovesick voice for beautiful Ann. For Patience she clapped her most ferocious scowl on her face and stamped her foot in rage.

Pops applauded when she was done and wiped tears of laughter from his eyes. "You're better than the theater, Lindy," he said. "You're a regular little actress."

Lindy knew that Pops was exaggerating, but she didn't mind. She felt the happiest she had since Joan went away.

Gram bustled in with another pile of strips, and Lindy groaned. The magical world of the Pilgrim play receded, and it was just another boring Saturday.

Gram eyed her sharply. "First you say you're bored, then when I find something for you to do you complain about it," she said, depositing the strips in Lindy's workbasket. "Of course you needn't do them if you haven't a mind to, but don't just sit around all day moping."

"Lindy's been telling me about her school play," Pops said. "You should see her act, Mother."

"Well, that's very nice," Gram said. "I don't remember hearing anything about a play."

"It's nothing," Lindy said.

"Now, don't you believe her, Mother. It's a fine play."

"I'm sure it is," Gram said, and went back to cutting.

Lindy looked down at her basket, overflowing with strips, each one to sew by hand with tiny little stitches.

Light ones and dark ones, pink, lavender, purple—she recognized the pink as one of Joan's old summer nighties, too worn to be handed down. The material had little pink ballet shoes all over it. Ballet shoes for dancing on the real stage in New York.

She scuffed impatiently at the rug with her stocking feet, wishing she hadn't told Pops about the play. Now he'd be so disappointed that she wasn't even going to try out for it. She scuffed harder, and a sharp pinprick stabbed into her right foot. The lost needle was found. Lindy reached down and pulled it from her thick wool sock, threaded it again, and began to sew, one stitch and then another, and another, and another.

The auditions were to be Monday, right after lunch. Meg spent the whole bus ride to school talking about them. Lindy fidgeted and stared out the window and pretended not to be listening, but Meg didn't take the hint very well. She kept on talking. Meg wanted the part of Ann, but Alice was trying out for Ann, too. Lindy thought that Mrs. Adams would have to pick Alice over Meg if there was any justice in the world. But she didn't say that to Meg.

Lindy knew that Nan wanted the part of Patience, and though she tried not to care about it, it bothered her. If Lindy wasn't going to try out, there was no reason Nan shouldn't get the best part. Somebody had to. But Lindy had seen Nan scowl, and her own scowl was infinitely better. Nan always looked as if she were about to burst out laughing.

As the morning dragged on, Lindy wondered how Mrs. Adams would react when it came time for the auditions and she refused to try out. Would she give a kindly, understanding smile and feel sorry that Lindy was too shy to act in front of all the others? Maybe she would be angry and tell Lindy that the whole class had to try out, whether they wanted to or not. Lindy might be sent to the principal in disgrace. Or maybe Mrs. Adams would coax her to read just one scene, just a few lines. Lindy would finally give in and agree to try the scene with the pies. How she would scowl! "You merely thought, did you?!" But, no, Lindy wasn't going to think about that.

When the auditions finally began, Nan volunteered to go first. She read the pie scene with Mickey Acton, the shortest boy in the class. Mickey made a perfect meek John, stammering timidly that no one had given him leave to touch the pies. But Nan read her lines too fast, and she still looked like she thought they were funny. Lindy didn't like that at all. The audience was supposed to decide whether or not Patience was funny.

Meg was even worse, though, as Ann. Sitting in the middle of the classroom, Lindy could hardly hear her, and Meg delivered all her lines in a monotonous singsong: "'So, CAPtain, WERE you MUCH aFRAID at SEA?'"

The part of Ann would have to go to Alice, with her high, clear voice and beautiful blond curls. Tommy Tillson was the best for the peglegged Captain's part. His limp was so real that Lindy could almost believe he had lost a leg at sea. He was the only boy, too, who was as tall as Alice, and that had to count for something.

"Who hasn't gone yet?" Mrs. Adams asked, looking down at her sheet of names. "Walter Johnson is absent today, so I'm afraid we'll have to cast this play without him. Lindy, you haven't read any part yet. Which would you like to try out for?"

Lindy took a deep breath. "I don't want to be in the play." There, she had said it.

Mrs. Adams looked puzzled. "Are you sure? I don't want to force anyone to take a part, but I think it's a very valuable experience."

All Lindy had to do was to act the least bit hesitant or shy, and Mrs. Adams would urge her one more time. But for some reason Lindy couldn't make herself give in.

"I'm sure," she said, feeling her heart swell inside her tight chest.

"All right, then, class, let's have silent reading for the next ten minutes, and then I'll announce the cast."

Wait! Lindy longed to cry out. *I want to be in the play more than anything!* But she just sat there, numb and silent. She couldn't believe that the auditions were over and no one had seen her bellow or waddle; no one had seen her cuff John's ears and scowl. She sat perfectly still, in silent misery. The play was the only thing in Three Churches that she could have cared about, and she had deliberately thrown it away.

Lindy's book was propped open in front of her, but she didn't read a word. No one else was reading, either. Nan was doodling on the cover of her spelling book. Alice drummed nervously on her desk.

Finally Mrs. Adams looked up. "Now, class," she said, "before I announce the cast, I want to remind you all once more that everyone who doesn't get a part will have an equally important job on one of the backstage committees.

The work that people do behind the scenes is just as important as what happens onstage."

Then she picked up her copy of the play. "The cast, in order of appearance: John—Mickey Acton; the Captain—Tommy Tillson; Ann—Alice Miller; Patience—Nan Daniels . . ." Mrs. Adams read on down the list, committees and all. Meg was one of the Pilgrim women. Lindy was in charge of props.

The bell rang. Lindy forced herself not to cry in front of everyone. Smiling with all her might, she took her place in line and marched outside with the rest of the class. But as the others filed onto the waiting buses, Lindy kept on walking—through the schoolyard and past the Presbyterian church, past Bowker's Feed and Necker Brothers, where Pops would never work again.

By the time she reached the old fairgrounds, she was almost running. What if the door was locked this time, the way all the other doors had been? But, no, it creaked open when she pushed against it, and the carousel was still there. The afternoon sun spilled through the high windows across the worn faces of the silent animals.

Lindy climbed onto the carousel and walked over to the giraffe. With a sob, she pulled herself up onto his comfortable broad back and threw her arms around his cracked neck. The tears trickled down her face, dropping onto the painted wood. But the giraffe didn't seem to mind. He stood patiently still, consoling her without a word, as Lindy held fast to his neck and cried.

NINE

"Did you get the part?" Pops asked as Lindy trudged slowly up the front porch steps. He probably waited for her to come home from school the way he waited for the mail.

Lindy didn't answer until she had flopped down beside Pops on the creaky old porch swing. "No," she said, avoiding Pops's eyes. "She gave it to Nan."

"No kidding!" Pops sounded so disappointed that Lindy was afraid she might cry again. "So which one are you going to be? The one who runs off to marry the Captain?"

"Ann," Lindy supplied. "Alice is going to be Ann."

Pops started to guess again, but Lindy stopped him. "I'm in charge of props."

"Well, now, that's a lot of responsibility, isn't it?" He was trying hard to make it sound as if props were something nice, instead of the single most boring committee of the whole play.

"I guess so."

Lindy didn't know if Pops would feel better or worse if she told him the truth about the auditions. He had put so much faith in her acting that it wasn't fair to let him think she had tried and failed. But she couldn't really explain her refusal to try out without explaining everything she had felt inside for the last few weeks. And Pops looked so old and tired today, as if he didn't feel well, or something.

Lindy looked at him more closely. It was Pops's mouth that looked funny, that was it. He had moved it stiffly when he spoke, as if it hurt him to talk. She edged nearer to him on the swing. "Is anything the matter?" she asked.

"I had another appointment with Doctor Graves." Doctor Graves was the dentist. "It's been years since I've had more'n six teeth of my own upstairs, and now two of them have gone bad. Happens they're the two that hold onto my fancy bridgework up front."

"Can he fix it?"

"Well, Graves figures the time has come to pull out the lot of them."

Lindy tried to imagine Pops without any of his teeth. She felt sick to her stomach at the thought.

"He's going to fix me a set of dentures. I should have them by the end of the week. But right now I only have half as many teeth as I did this morning."

Poor Pops. Lindy's teeth ached for him. "Maybe you should go lie down," she suggested. Pops's face looked taut with pain.

"That's not a half-bad idea, Lindy," Pops said. He stood up slowly from the swing. "So what kind of props are you in charge of?"

"I don't know yet. There's a gun, I think. And the pies."

"Just let me know how I can help, honey." He hesitated for a moment. "And don't give up on your acting, promise? Your teacher probably figured all those other kids needed more of a break than someone with a God-given talent like yours."

When Pops went inside Lindy stayed on the swing, creaking rhythmically back and forth. Through her sadness over the props committee and Pops's dentures flickered a small spark of hope. It was a new idea to Lindy that she, too, might have a talent that shouldn't be hidden away. Of course, Pops loved her so much that he thought everything she did was wonderful and amazing, and you didn't have to be much of an actress to read lines better than Nan or Meg. Still, Lindy knew that her scowl *had* been something special. She would never hide her talent under a bushel again.

As head of the props committee, Lindy's job was to find a big iron pot to hang in the Pilgrim fireplace, assorted bowls and plates, an old-fashioned musket, a bucket, and two pumpkin pies. The bowls and plates should be unbreakable; the pies—Patience's pies—shouldn't be real pies that would spoil before the rehearsals were through.

The day Lindy brought her list home, Pops retired to his basement shop after supper. Lindy could hear the buzz of the power saw and the pounding of the hammer. Every once in a while Pops came upstairs, smiling mysteriously, only to disappear back to the basement again. When Pops smiled, Lindy could see his gleaming white set of temporary dentures. They were all perfectly white and uniform, like a movie star's teeth.

Gram looked up from her lapful of log cabin squares and shook her head. "Bless my heart, I don't know when I've seen him take to a project like this."

"He doesn't have to help me if his mouth hurts," Lindy said. Pops had hardly eaten any supper, even though Gram had made sure there was nothing hard or tough or stringy.

"He loves it," Gram said. "I wish he had a project like this one every night. You, too, young lady. The two of you are a pair."

Lindy guiltily picked up her needle. She didn't like being compared to Pops, who spent every evening rocking back and forth in his chair as Gram sewed or knitted or sorted through the mending pile. Her grandparents hardly ever watched TV, other than the evening news, and neither of them was much for reading books or magazines. But Gram's fingers were always busy making something useful or beautiful, while Pops just waited for the slow hands of the clock to creep around to bedtime, at nine-thirty or ten. Often Lindy had homework to do at the kitchen table. But otherwise she was almost as bad as Pops. She couldn't get interested in a book when the house was so quiet and the clock ticked so loudly. And after half a dozen seams she would lay down her needle and watch the rapid, deft motion of Gram's fingers as her eyelids grew heavier and heavier. Was she as boring as Pops? Energetically, Lindy pinned two more strips together and began stitching in earnest.

"Pie, anyone?" Pops's loud voice gave Lindy a start. Pops was grinning mischievously around the door.

"What in the world—" Gram began as Pops held out two perfectly formed pumpkin pies.

"But they're not supposed to be real," Lindy said, confused.

"Have a piece," Pops said slyly.

He brought them closer, so Lindy could tell they were made of wood, stained pumpkin-color, with a crimped crust of fluted sawdust and glue.

"Oh, Pops," Lindy said, "they're beautiful."

"They look pretty darned real, if I do say so myself." Pops carried them over to Gram. "What do you say, Mother?"

Gram nodded in approval. "Well, you still do have the knack, I have to say that."

Lindy stared at the pies in fascination. The play would be wonderful with magnificent wooden pies like these for props. True, the pies were to be Nan's pies, not hers. Nan would be the one to waddle back and forth with them, not Lindy. But there would be other plays, Mrs. Adams had said so. And when there were, Lindy's talent would shine forth, and Pops would be so proud and pleased.

"It's getting on to bedtime for you, Lindy," Gram said. "The pies will still be here when you wake up."

Lindy kissed Gram and Pops good night. She gave the pies one last, loving look and went off to bed.

TEN

The weeks before the play passed quickly, and Lindy realized with surprise that she was enjoying school more than she would have believed possible back in September. In October they studied fractions, just as Lindy had known they would. Joan's coaching paid off royally, and Lindy tied for the class prize with Tommy Tillson. She didn't care about bringing in the class pumpkin, but it was satisfying to be the best at something—well, tied for the best. Maybe Lindy had two talents—acting and fractions. Of course, fractions didn't come up in real life very often, but being good at them was fun.

The first week in November they sent away for pen pals. Lindy hoped her pen pal would be from Andorra, but Mrs. Adams told her that she should put down some other countries as well. The class had just seen a filmstrip on Holland, so Lindy picked Holland, too. A Dutch pen pal would have very blond hair, not dirty blond like Lindy's. She would wear wooden shoes and go skating in the winter on long canals lined with windmills. But Lindy still wanted a pen pal from Andorra the most.

On Wednesday afternoons, Mrs. Adams took the whole class to the library to do research on their Nations of the World projects. Lindy was in love with all her little countries and treasured every fact about them. One principal industry of Liechtenstein was selling postage stamps! And Monaco had been ruled by a princess who had once been a famous American movie star.

Lindy imagined a similar future for Joan. Any day some fabulously wealthy and handsome prince might see one of her ballets, if not now, then surely during Joan's company tour abroad. Lindy wrote Joan all about it, but Joan was busy with constant classes and rehearsals, and her letters came less often.

For Gram and Pops's sake, Lindy wished Joan would write more, but Joan's letters always made Lindy cross and dissatisfied. Lindy would just be feeling pleased about the fractions prize when a letter would come filled with a list of Joan's exciting adventures: nights at the theater, a ferry ride to Staten Island, afternoon tea at the Plaza Hotel. Lindy had never seen a play or ridden on a ferry. Probably Gram and Pops hadn't, either. And tea in the kitchen at home was as ordinary as anything could be. It seemed to Lindy that life's excitement should be divided more equally.

The play was becoming exciting, though. It wasn't going to be held in the classroom after all, but in the school auditorium, with the fourth grade and sixth grade as the audience. All the parents were invited, too. Gram and Pops had been looking forward to going ever since Pops made the pies. They couldn't wait to see how real and edible they would look on the stage.

The pies looked absolutely real on Mrs. Adams's desk, where she had left them for all the class to admire. The teacher had been speechless with amazement when Lindy proudly carried them in to school, along with Pops's painted plywood musket. "I can see we picked the right person for the props committee!" she had said, and Lindy's boring assignment had had its moment of glory.

Lindy had the pies backstage now, with the other props. It was her job to give them to Patience before her second scene entrance. Later in the play, she had to make sure they were safely offstage again, ready to make their final appearance in the crucial scene. Lindy had butterflies in her stomach thinking about all she had to remember— what if she forgot to hand the Captain his musket and he stormed onstage empty-handed? Then the play would be ruined, and it would be all her fault.

But she didn't forget, and the play was a success. Even backstage, Lindy could hear the laughter and applause. Alice needed to be prompted twice, Tommy made his first entrance late, and in the final scene the Pilgrim cabin came close to toppling over. None of it seemed to matter. The audience stomped its feet and whistled for more.

Lindy knew they could have been stomping and whistling for her, if only she had been a little less stubborn a month ago. She imagined herself curtseying again and again as the audience kept on clapping, with Gram and Pops beaming at her from the very first row. But next time she would be the star, she promised herself. Three

Churches wasn't Broadway, but even in Three Churches it was better to be the star than to be in charge of props. She knew that now.

Mrs. Adams had invited all the parents to have punch and cookies in the fifth-grade classroom after the play. Nan and Alice looked funny eating thick fudge brownies in Pilgrim costume, their garish theatrical makeup still on. Nan had removed her pillows, and her costume billowed about her.

"You were terrific, both of you," Lindy said. She felt generous now, basking in the play's success. She no longer felt jealous that none of the applause and laughter had been for her. Actually, the applause was for the entire play, and she and Pops *had* been an important part of it, like Mrs. Adams had said.

"Where is your grandfather, Lindy?" Mrs. Adams asked, coming up behind her with a plate of cookies. "I want to thank him for all his help on the props committee."

Lindy signaled to Gram and Pops, who had just come in the classroom door. Pops was wearing the same jacket he had worn for the Necker Brothers banquet, and Gram had on a new cranberry-colored dress. Lindy felt proud of both of them.

"We can't thank you enough for your assistance with our props," Mrs. Adams told Pops. "I think your beautiful pies just about stole the show."

"Well, I'm always glad when I'm able to help out," Pops said. "If you think you'll be using them in other shows, you're welcome to keep them."

"Why, thank you," Mrs. Adams said. "We'd love to keep them." She held out the tray of cookies, and Pops picked one of the chewy, moist, dark brownies.

"Homemade brownies," he said. "Nothing like them."

Or at least that's what he meant to say. The last words came out all garbled, and Lindy looked down at the brownie in horror. There, embedded in the sticky fudge, was the gleaming half-circle of Pops's upper teeth.

Mrs. Adams, after one quick glance, pretended not to notice. She thanked Pops again and bustled off to another cluster of parents. Gram hurriedly produced her handkerchief and wrapped up Pops's dentures before anyone else could see what had happened.

"It was a very nice play, Lindy, and all of you have a right to be proud," Gram said, firmly and brightly, steering Pops toward the door. "We'll see you back at home for supper."

Lindy stood stricken, unable to whisper a good-bye. She could never face Mrs. Adams again. This was worse than cheating herself out of the part of Patience. It was even worse than Joan's going away. Everything she had minded and resented for so long in Three Churches came together in that one terrible picture of Pops's dentures stuck in the half-chewed brownie. She closed her eyes, and all she could see were those fake white teeth gleaming in that gooey brown lump.

ELEVEN

"Have you seen him yet?" Gram called out from the kitchen. Lindy grimaced.

"Nope," Pops said from his post by the window. "Not a sign of him."

At least his dentures stayed in place when he said it, Lindy thought. None of them had mentioned that horrible, humiliating scene since it had happened, though Gram and Pops talked all the time about the play and how well the props had come off. Still, Lindy never looked at Pops without remembering.

"He should be here by now," Gram said, joining Pops by the window. "Maybe we missed him."

She checked the empty mailbox and shook her head. "He's later every day, he is."

"We never get any mail, anyway," Lindy said crossly. Pops looked over at her in mild surprise.

"Of course we do," he said. "Just think, maybe today there'll be a letter from your sister telling us when she's coming home for Thanksgiving."

"There he is," Gram announced, "down by Mitchells'. About time, too."

She bustled back to her gingerbread. The whole house was fragrant with cinnamon and cloves, so the loaves would be coming out of the oven soon. Gram's gingerbread was the county favorite at church dinners and fairs. Lindy, for one, was getting pretty tired of it.

They heard the click of the mailbox. "Do you want to get it, Lindy?" Pops asked. Getting the mail was supposed to be a big treat.

"You can do it," Lindy said.

When Pops opened the front door, the cold draft made Lindy shiver. They'd have a foot of snow by Christmas this year, for sure.

"What did I tell you? A letter from Joan! Mother, come on out here, there's a letter!"

Pops handed the letter to Lindy. She always read Joan's letters aloud, three or four times sometimes. She studied the envelope for a moment before she opened it. Joan had had little return address stickers printed with her New York address. They made her residence in New York seem so permanent and final.

The letter was written on the floral stationery Lindy had given her last Christmas, in Joan's tiny scrawl.

"'Dear Gram and Pops and Lindy,'" Lindy began. "'Something wonderful just happened. I've been pieced'—no, wait a minute, *picked*—'to be an apprentice at the City Ballet. This means that I'll be dancing with the company in the'"—Lindy squinted at the next word— "'*The Nutcracker*.'"

"Imagine that!" Pops said.

" 'It's a big horror'—I mean, *honor*—'to be accepted as an apprentice so young.' "

"I should say so," Pops inserted emphatically.

" 'The bad part is that now I won't be able to come home' "—the words stuck in Lindy's throat, but she made herself go on—" 'for Thanksgiving or Christmas. But I'll be thinking about all of you and missing you lots. . . .' "

There were two more pages, but Lindy couldn't bear to read them. She folded the letter carefully and slid it back into the envelope.

"You'd think they'd let her miss just one weekend," Pops said slowly. "I'm sure she can dance circles around all those other girls."

"Well, they can't," Lindy snapped. She had never heard Pops sound so defeated.

"When I think of how much I had set my heart on seeing her this month," Gram began, and trailed off. "Poor child, to have Thanksgiving dinner away from home."

"Aunt Bea's a gourmet cook, Joan said so," Lindy said. "It's not like she's all alone."

"Maybe she could come home just for Christmas day," Pops said. "It couldn't hurt to miss just one day."

"If she says she can't come home, she can't come home," Lindy said.

"I guess you're right." Pops looked down at his big, gnarled hands. "But we were so looking forward to having her back again."

It was cold and damp inside the carousel barn, but Lindy had put on an extra sweater under her hooded wool jacket. Thin sunlight trickled through the windows onto the seal's striped beach ball and the lion's shabby mane.

Lindy tried to imagine the carousel as it would have been fifty years ago. The paint had been bright and gay, and the animals had whirled about, faster and faster, keeping time to the calliope. There would have been a child perched on every one—old-fashioned children wearing short pants and sailor suits, like in Pops's faded photographs. Pops and Gram were young then, and Lindy's father hadn't even been born yet. Now he had been dead for years, and Gram and Pops were old. They were so old and they loved Joan so much, and she wasn't coming home for Christmas.

Lindy was so angry that she didn't even know where to put her rage. Well, she could start with Joan. Joan knew how much they all missed her, and she wouldn't cut a single rehearsal to fly home for one day. It was Joan's fault that Lindy had had to read that letter aloud and take away everything Gram and Pops had been looking forward to. Joan was like Benedict Arnold, that's who she was like. Lindy had learned about him last week in school: Benedict Arnold, the most famous traitor in American history, maybe even in the whole history of the world. Joan was a traitor, too. She was true to her dancing, all right, but she had betrayed Gram and Pops. And she had betrayed Lindy, who was left alone in boring, lonely Three Churches to take care of Gram and Pops all by herself.

But Lindy felt angry at Gram and Pops, too. They had no business letting her see how deeply disappointed Joan's letter had made them. Why couldn't they keep it to themselves and say something cheerful and comforting? It wasn't Lindy's fault that Pops sat all day waiting for the mail—it wasn't Joan's fault, either, for that matter. It probably wasn't even Pops's fault. It wasn't anybody's fault. But Lindy felt angry all the same. She shivered as the November wind whistled through the cracks in the old barn.

The carousel animals had nothing to say, and suddenly Lindy felt angrier at them than at Joan or anybody. For fifty years they had just *stood* there, while the children who had once gone for moonlit carousel rides grew up and had children of their own and moved away to Minneapolis and Des Moines and Chicago. The trains that had come through Three Churches had stopped coming, and the rusty railroad tracks where Lindy sometimes walked were overgrown with wildflowers and weeds. Everything in Three Churches had gotten older and slower and quieter, and the carousel animals hadn't done anything about it. They had just gotten older and slower and quieter, too.

Lindy walked over next to the giraffe and gazed up into his unseeing wooden eyes.

"I hate you," she said under her breath.

The giraffe said nothing.

"I hate you!" she said louder, and then, furious, she kicked at his spindly wooden legs. She blamed him for Pops's dentures and Joan's letter and all the cold, dreary months that stretched ahead from winter to spring.

She beat against the giraffe's cracked neck with her hard fists until her hands ached and she couldn't see through the tears in her eyes. Then, spent from anger, Lindy put her arms around the giraffe and hugged him close to her, overcome with remorse and sadness.

She knew now that she had made the wrong decision last summer at the fairgrounds. She couldn't stay in Three Churches any more than Joan could stay. One way or another, she would have to make her escape. She would plan all that later—the important thing was that she was going away; that, somehow, by the summer she would have said good-bye to Gram and Pops, to the carousel animals, to everything.

TWELVE

Would the tree be too tall for the living room ceiling? Pops said it wouldn't, Gram said it would, and Lindy skipped back and forth across the snowy porch with excitement. She had gone to the lot with Pops to pick it out, and it was the most beautiful tree they had ever had for any Christmas. The pick of the lot, Pops had said, as he had stood it firmly in the snow for Lindy's inspection. It was taller than Pops—but so was the ceiling—with its broad branches heavy with fragrant needles. Gram was helping Pops carry it out from the car, and they would trim it that afternoon. They always trimmed the tree on the weekend before Christmas.

"We can cut off some of those bottom boughs for greens," Gram said, shaking her head doubtfully as they maneuvered it through the door.

"It'll fit just fine," Pops said. "Wait and see."

The armchair and side table had been cleared away from the big front window, and Gram had spread clear plastic over that portion of the rug to protect it from shedding needles. Pops carried the tree over to the place of honor and tipped it into the wooden base. Slowly, he raised it upright. The top of the tree cleared the ceiling by an inch.

"What did I tell you?" Pops said.

He pushed down gently on the branches, which had been tied together tightly in the lot, and they all stepped back to admire. Lindy felt a lump in her throat. It was her first Christmas without Joan, and it might be her last Christmas with Gram and Pops. If she was in New York next year, she might not be able to come home, either. She took a deep breath and filled her lungs with the spicy, woodsy smell of balsam.

While Pops strung the colored lights around the branches, Lindy and Gram climbed up to the attic for the boxes of ornaments. Gram and Pops had ornaments that had belonged to *their* grandparents, as well as box after box they had collected together throughout their marriage.

Lindy's favorites were the family of little straw animals and the six shiny, fat Santas. They were the first ones she put up every year. Joan always took care of the carved wooden angels and the golden trumpets and horns.

"I wonder if Bea is having a tree for Joan," Gram said, handing Lindy the box of Santas.

"I don't reckon folks bother as much with Christmas in the city," Pops said from his perch on the stepladder. It was Pops's job to place the tinfoil star way up on the very highest branch.

"Of course they do," Gram said. "They have that great big tree up at Rockefeller Center, the one Joan sent us the postcard of."

The mailman had brought them the postcard yesterday, and Lindy felt hurt and angry whenever she thought about it. That New York City tree could be two miles tall, for all she cared. As if their own little tree with Gram and Pops wasn't infinitely more beautiful. Next year she wouldn't even look at the Rockefeller Center tree. She would walk right past it as if it didn't even exist.

"You always put them up first," Gram said. Lindy had laid aside the box of Santas.

Forcing a bright smile, she lifted off the top of the box. The Santas were as chubby and shiny as ever. She hung the first one somewhere in the middle of the tree, and his big red belly twinkled at her merrily.

Once the star was in place, Gram began handing Pops ornaments for the top branches. One by one, Joan's golden horns and trumpets glistened against the dark evergreen needles, and her wooden angels swung gracefully as if hovering in flight.

The straw animals had come all the way from Sweden, with Gram's grandparents in the 1800s. Lindy liked the idea of touching something from so long ago and far away. And this year the little straw horse made her think of the horse on the secret carousel. She made sure to place the little horse deep in the branches, in his own secret hiding place.

When all the ornaments were hung, Gram and Pops draped handfuls of tinsel all over the tree. It was Lindy's job to crawl on the floor retrieving fallen strands, so that not a one would be wasted. She wondered if the big tree at Rockefeller Center could possibly have tinsel all over it, too. She imagined driving back and forth collecting stray tinsel in an enormous trailer truck.

Finally, Pops turned off the table lamps and switched on the tree lights. Red, yellow, blue, and green lights made the tinsel shimmer and the dozens of ornaments seem to dance.

The last Christmas.

Every Christmas, Gram made five kinds of Christmas cookies. This year she let Lindy invite Nan and Alice to help with the gingerbread boys. The dough was made and chilled the night before so it would roll out easily for cutting. Every once in a while Lindy would peek in the refrigerator to see if it was still there—a smooth round lump wrapped in foil.

Gram was in charge of the rolling, and the girls took turns with the cookie cutters. They had to cut out five dozen cookies, all to be decorated with raisin eyes and cinnamon candy buttons.

"My mother says she's never tasted better gingerbread than yours, Mrs. Webster," Alice said as the second tray went into the oven. Alice always knew how to talk to grown-ups.

"Well, I've had some fifty years of practice now, since I was your age," Gram said.

Nan popped a scrap of dough into her mouth while Gram wasn't looking and went on cutting innocently. "They'll taste even better than those pumpkin pies did in the play," she said. "Right, Mr. Webster?" Pops had strolled into the kitchen in hopes of a first sample.

"I sure hope so," Pops said, grinning.

"Wait till they're decorated," Gram said, "and you can have all you want."

"All right, Mother, if you say so." Pops slyly snapped the foot off one of the boys from the first batch, while Nan and Lindy giggled. "But this one here's broken, so no point icing it." He winked broadly at them.

"Are you going to make popcorn balls this year?" Nan asked him. Popcorn balls were Pops's holiday specialty.

"I don't know. Just a few, maybe. I have some false teeth upstairs now, and popcorn balls'd stick to them like the devil. Right, Lindy?"

He smiled at Lindy, and she knew he wanted her to smile back, to let him know she didn't mind about the brownie at the play. The scene came back to her so vividly that she felt her face growing hot and red. She wasn't going to smile about it, however Pops might feel. It was nothing to joke about, and especially not in front of Nan and Alice. Grimly, she stuck two raisin eyes in the first gingerbread boy's blank face. The second raisin was crooked, giving the boy a quizzical, cross-eyed look.

But it was Christmas, and Pops stood looking at her expectantly. If she didn't look up and smile at him now, next Christmas she would still remember that she hadn't.

Lindy glanced up tentatively with a small smile. Pops's smile grew even wider, and Lindy found her own stretching to match his. And then they were both laughing. Lindy imagined the dentures stuck fast in the popcorn ball, as if the Cheshire Cat's grin from *Alice in Wonderland* were trying to eat all by itself. She laughed until her stomach hurt, and Pops laughed until he needed to pull out his handkerchief to wipe away the tears.

"I'm sure I don't know what's supposed to be so funny," Gram said. "Of course dental work would stick to popcorn balls."

At Gram's words, Pops and Lindy went off again in gales of helpless laughter. Nan and Alice smiled politely, not understanding the joke.

"You're a pair, the two of you." Gram pushed the bowl of raisins closer to Lindy's tray of eyeless boys.

"I guess we are that, Mother," Pops said, reaching down to tug at Lindy's pigtail. "I guess you could say we are."

It snowed on Christmas Eve, so instead of going to church, Lindy read the Christmas story from the Bible to Gram and Pops at home. Usually Joan, as the older sister, had done all the reading aloud, but Lindy put more expression in what she read. She tried to put in her voice the fear of the shepherds and the glory of the heavenly host. When she finished, Gram and Pops both bowed their heads and she said amen, just as if she had been a real minister in church.

Then she set up the manger scene, which she and Joan had always done together. Each porcelain figure was wrapped in newspaper, and the two of them used to make a ceremony of unwrapping the pieces one by one, to see who got Joseph and Mary and baby Jesus in his little wooden crib full of straw. The best pieces to get were the donkey and the pinkish white king.

For years there had been two black kings and one white one. Then, four Christmases ago, Joan had come home from Sunday school and informed Gram that there were supposed to be two white kings and one black one. Gram had had Pops paint the second black king an odd pinkish white, and each year when they unwrapped him, Joan and Lindy practically rolled on the floor laughing. But this year Lindy unwrapped all the pieces herself, and the pinkish white king only made her smile. That was the saddest part of Christmas without Joan.

In spite of Joan's absence, Lindy awoke on Christmas morning with the usual stirrings of joy. She could hardly wait to give Gram and Pops their presents. Gram's was an apron done in cross-stitch embroidery, which Lindy had managed to keep a secret for all the weeks she had worked on it. For Pops, Lindy had a ceramic ashtray she had made in art class on Tuesdays, and a book of comic epitaphs she had bought when Nan's parents took them Christmas shopping in Middleton. Pops didn't smoke, but he could use the ashtray to hold spare change when he emptied his pockets at night. She even had a present for Shep—a king-sized box of dog biscuits.

They never opened presents until after breakfast, so Lindy gobbled down Gram's homemade yeast coffeecake as quickly as she could, not asking for seconds. Pops didn't waste any time on his breakfast, either, and Gram was willing to leave the table without clearing away the dishes.

There was a tremendous pile of presents, even without Joan's, which had been mailed off to her in a giant carton weeks ago. Joan's presents for them had arrived last week, and they alone took up half the space under the tree. Of course, some of the presents from Gram and Pops would be boring things like underwear and galoshes, but there was still a great pile to open.

An hour later Lindy sat surrounded by treasures. Joan had sent her a funny stuffed chipmunk and a book on how to do magic tricks. Wouldn't Meg O'Neill be surprised when Lindy calmly made quarters disappear into thin air during bus rides to and from school! Aunt Bea had sent her a pretty yellow sweater and a box of watercolor paints. From Gram and Pops there were a new pair of ice skates, a wicker sewing basket, and piles of clothes.

Best of all, though, was watching Gram and Pops open their presents. Gram immediately shed her old apron and tied Lindy's around her waist, marveling at all the tiny stitches. Lindy had known Gram would look at the wrong side, so she had taken care that the stitches on the back were as neat as those on the front.

"You've done yourself proud, Lindy," Gram said.

Pops couldn't get over his ashtray. He studied it from all angles and demonstrated its many uses for storing coins, keys, bits of twine, all the while shaking his head in disbelief. The book of epitaphs made him laugh almost as much as the popcorn balls had. "I told you I was sick" was his favorite, though Gram didn't think it was as funny as he did. And Shep lay in a great pile of Christmas paper and ribbon, gnawing contentedly on his biscuits.

There was still one package left under the tree, a big square box wrapped in red tissue paper with a white bow.

"This one's for you, honey," Pops said, handing it to her shyly.

Lindy carefully peeled off the wrapping and slowly lifted the top off the box, wondering what it could be. She had gotten so many presents already. Inside was crumpled tissue paper.

"Go ahead," Pops said, grinning at Gram.

Lindy fumbled in the paper and pulled out a family of wooden dolls—a father, a mother, a big sister, and a little brother—beautifully handcarved and painted. Their arms and legs were jointed, so the dolls could sit and bend; each hand had five perfectly carved little fingers; and each foot had five tiny toes. But best of all were the expressions on their faces: the father so kind and serious, the little brother smiling shyly.

Lindy looked up at Pops in bewilderment. There could be no other dolls like these anywhere in the world.

"He made them," Gram explained. Lindy stared back at the dolls again, overcome by happiness. "Do you like them?" Gram asked. Pops looked at her anxiously.

"They're beautiful," Lindy said. She remembered to get up and give Pops a big kiss. "They're beautiful," she said again. "I love them, I do."

"Your Pops has a real talent," Gram said. "Though I think he forgot all about it until you needed that pie."

"Merry Christmas, honey," Pops said, smiling at her pleasure.

"Merry Christmas, Pops," Lindy said.

THIRTEEN

Usually the weeks following Christmas were long and dull. Gram and Pops took down the tree on New Year's Eve, and it lay next to the woodshed for the rest of the winter, with a few forgotten strands of tinsel clinging to the bare branches. The tins of Christmas cookies were emptied one by one, and Gram announced that it was time to "go easy on desserts" for a while. Pops's seed catalogs came in the mail, but it seemed impossible that it would be planting time again.

This year, though, on the day after vacation, Mrs. Adams announced the second class play, *The Golden Touch*. It was the story of greedy King Midas, who wishes that everything he touches would turn to gold. The gods grant his wish, and at first the king is overjoyed to be able to turn common objects into priceless treasures. But then he sees that even his food and drink turn into gold when he raises them to his lips. Finally, he kisses his beloved daughter, Marigold, and before his very eyes she turns into a golden statue. Horrified, King Midas begs the gods to take away his golden touch, and they take pity on him, since he has been cured of his greediness at last.

The best girl's part was Marigold. It would be hard to stand completely still, without moving a single muscle, but Lindy knew she could do it. No one would even be able to see her breathe. The other girl's parts were good, too: the king's grieving wife, the jolly nursemaid, the haughty ladies in the royal court. But Marigold was the part Lindy planned on getting.

The tryouts were going to be a week from Wednesday. Lindy told Shep about them, but not Gram or Pops. This time she wasn't going to tell Pops until the part was hers.

"So do you think I'd be good as Marigold?" she asked Shep, laying her head against his.

Shep thumped his tail once against the floor. Once meant yes, Lindy decided. She concentrated on her breathing, trying not to let her chest rise or fall as she stared straight ahead, glassy-eyed. She held the pose as long as she could and then threw her arms around the old dog.

"Did I fool you, Shep? Did you think I was a statue?"

One more thump. Lindy knew she could always count on Shep.

It was warmer for a few days, and Lindy walked through the snow after school to the carousel. All she wanted to do lately was practice Marigold's part, and the carousel was an ideal place to rehearse. There was lots of room, and she could make all the noise she wanted.

And Marigold's biggest scene was *very* noisy. The little princess loves flowers and spends hours in her own special garden outside the royal palace. Her father goes there to pick her a pretty nosegay, but as he touches each flower it turns into a stiff, lifeless thing. When Marigold sees her sweet flowers turned metallic and cold, she throws herself upon the grass, heartbroken.

"'My flowers! My beautiful flowers!'" Lindy flung herself upon the worn floor next to the carousel. Her wild sobbing frightened the birds perched high on a beam beneath the barn rafters.

"'Oh, Father, how I hate them now!'"

Lindy felt herself drawn up into the king's arms to be comforted. But it was too late. She froze instantly, a statue of solid gold.

So still she stood, her face caught in the contortion of crying. The startled birds flapped about in the shadowy eaves and, hearing no more sudden shrieks, settled back in their resting place.

It seemed that Lindy stood there a long time without moving. Then, slowly, she came back to life again.

All the girls wanted to be Marigold. Nan, Alice, and Meg all thought it was the best part, though Nan said she wouldn't mind being the nursemaid. No one asked Lindy which part she wanted. They just assumed that because she had refused to try out the last time, she would refuse this time, too. It was hard for Lindy to believe that no one in the class knew that she could act. Only Shep and Pops had seen her talent shine out from under its bushel.

On the day of the tryouts, Lindy wore her first-day-of-school blue jumper, the one that matched her eyes. She knew that if she really truly had a talent for acting, she should be able to make the class believe that her old overalls with the patches on the knees were a cloak of purple velvet, edged with ermine. But it would be easier to make them believe it if she wore her best jumper. Her golden crown would have to be purely imaginary, though. As Lindy waited for the bus she held her head higher, conscious of its weight.

It took even longer for afternoon to come this time than it had for the last auditions, but finally Mrs. Adams asked them to clear off the tops of their desks and get their scripts ready.

"Who wants to go first?" Mrs. Adams asked. Lindy had already decided not to volunteer. She would make more of a sensation by going last.

Nan put up her hand, and Mrs. Adams called on Tommy Tillson to read with her, as King Midas. Lindy felt her heart pounding as Nan read Marigold's lines, but Nan was no better as Marigold than she had been as Patience. Her tantrum was okay, though she seemed *mad* rather than heartbroken, but her statue couldn't stand still without laughing.

Alice made a beautiful Marigold, and her statue froze almost as convincingly as Lindy's. But Alice didn't know the first thing about having a tantrum. That was what happened when you spent your whole life being sweet and good. Meg failed in Lindy's eyes in both statue and tantrum departments, and none of the other girls were any better.

"Any other volunteers?" Mrs. Adams asked then, looking over at Lindy with a smile of encouragement.

Lindy gave a small nod.

"Good for you! Now, are there any boys who haven't gone? No? Would you mind reading again, Tommy?"

Tommy was clearly the best of the boys, so that was a stroke of luck. Lindy waited until he took his place in the front of the classroom, and then slowly started up from her seat.

"Don't forget your script," she heard Mrs. Adams say.

But Lindy didn't need the script. "'My flowers! My beautiful flowers!'" she sobbed, rushing up to where the king, her father, stood waiting. Unmindful of her best jumper, she threw herself on the classroom floor, flailing her legs and arms against the cold linoleum.

"'But, my child—'" Tommy stammered, taken aback by the violence of her grief.

"'Oh, Father, how I hate them now!'" Lindy cried. "'Oh, Father, how I hate them!'"

The king drew her up into his arms. She froze. He knelt beside her lifeless form. And then Lindy was startled to hear the sound of applause.

They were all clapping, and they were clapping for *her*. Nan and Alice beamed triumphant smiles, and even Mrs. Adams joined in the applause. Lindy hurried back to her seat, red with embarrassment and pride.

The casting announcements came as no surprise to anyone. Tommy was King Midas, Alice was the queen, Nan was the funny nursemaid, and Lindy Webster was Marigold, the girl's lead, the best girl's part in the best play Three Churches would ever see produced.

Lindy thought long and hard about all this as she walked to the carousel after school. It was too cold to go there, really, since the temperature had dropped into the teens, and more snow was forecast for that night. But she had taken all her sadness and disappointment to the carousel animals; they deserved to share her triumphs, too.

The dry snow crunched under her boots as she walked the familiar route. Bowker's feed silos were capped with stiff white peaks of frozen meringue, and Necker's display tractors were half-buried in the drifts. But the carousel animals were safe and dry, and the snow that drifted up against the old barn made it warmer inside.

Never before in Lindy's life had so much attention and praise come her way. The applause had always been for Joan. But now she had been the one onstage, and everyone had seen that she had a talent, too. She huddled against the giraffe for warmth, looking up at his sweet, sad face.

She had vowed before Thanksgiving to leave Three Churches, and now she knew how to do it. *The Golden Touch* would be so magnificent that everyone would see that she had to go right to Broadway. Lindy remembered when Joan's ballet teacher had first told Gram and Pops that Joan's gift needed the kind of special training Three Churches could never provide. She imagined Mrs. Adams telling them the same thing about her after the play. Pops would write to Aunt Bea, and everything would be settled. Lindy would be rushed to the airport, on her way to New York. She shivered with anticipation.

Pops was waiting by the window for her when she reached home, as the first flakes began to whirl through the falling darkness.

"We were starting to get worried, honey," he said, brushing the snow from her hooded jacket.

"Guess what?" Lindy asked him.

"What?"

"Guess who has the lead in the next class play?"

"Well, I bet I can guess, too! See what I told you? Mother, come out here—we have an actress in the family!"

Lindy glowed with pleasure. It wasn't just for her own sake that she had wanted to be Marigold. It was for Pops, to, who had seen her talent when no one else had—Pops, who was so proud of his two girls. Even as she stood telling him about the play, with the words tumbling one after another, she felt a twinge of sadness. Pops was so proud of her talent and Joan's, but it was their talents that would take them away from him.

FOURTEEN

Lindy lay on her stomach in front of the fireplace, watching the last fiery fragments of wood smolder and glow. The embers seemed to form a fantastic underground city, all radiantly lit by ten thousand lanterns. She picked up the poker and gingerly nudged the last log, sending whirlwinds of sparks up the blackened chimney. It was nice to lie on Gram's braided rug, staring into the grate, as the snow outside drifted deeper and deeper.

It had been snowing off and on since Wednesday, and by now, Sunday, twenty-one inches had fallen. Pops listened to the snow accumulation every hour on the weather report, and this morning he had announced that they were snowed in. The snow had blown so deep against the back door that they couldn't push it open, and the North Post Road was lost, obscured completely by now. No one had driven by for hours, which showed Pops that folks had some sense, after all.

"I thought you'd like some cocoa," Gram said, setting a fat mug beside Lindy on the rug. The cocoa was made

Lindy's favorite way, too, with little marshmallows floating in it.

"Thanks, Gram."

"And I thought you'd like some sugar cookies." From behind her back Gram produced a plate of cookies, hot from the oven. Lindy grinned up at her gratefully and took a giant bite out of the first one.

Gram looked over at Pops, dozing in his armchair by the window, and shook her head. Gram never took naps. "He'll have to eat his cookies after they've cooled," she said, pronouncing Pop's punishment, and bustled back to take care of the second batch.

Lindy nibbled dreamily on her cookies, gnawing neatly all around the outside before she allowed herself to bite into the soft center. The glowing ember city kept shifting and changing as the embers burned themselves into different configurations. She began to pretend that the city was New York, lit up after dark with millions of lights in millions of windows. One ember was Aunt Bea's apartment, where she would live next year with Joan. And, there, that little cluster of embers, that was Broadway, the Great White Way.

But what was Pops going to do when she was gone? That was the question that worried Lindy most. She needed to think of more projects for Pops to do, more plywood pies to make, or more carved wooden dolls. Maybe when she was an actress in New York she could ask Pops to make the props for all her plays. That would be an exciting project, all right.

There was a pile of old newspapers beside the fireplace, and Lindy laid one of last week's sports sections on the fire, watching it burst suddenly into leaping flames. Beneath it in the pile lay Pops's seed catalogs. Lindy took the top one and flipped idly through the glossy photographs of ripe, red tomatoes. She couldn't believe that there could be so many kinds of tomatoes in the world. They looked so red and shiny that it was a shame to burn their pictures in the fire. And the lettuce so crisp and green, the eggplants so sleek and purple—Lindy should cut out some of them for her scrapbook.

The clock on the mantel struck four, and Pops opened his eyes. "Guess I dozed off for a bit," he said to Lindy.

He got up heavily and looked out the window at the Mitchells' cornfields, lying beneath the cloudy sky and the drifted snow. Sky and snow were the same grayish white in the half-light of late afternoon. "Snow's stopped," he said. "I wouldn't be surprised if there's been two more inches this afternoon, though. Must be two feet out there now."

Lindy turned the pages to look at the corn. Iowa had had the prize harvest last year, but Illinois had been a too-close second for Lindy's comfort. If only Pops grew corn! For every little bit helped.

The more Lindy stared at the corn photographs, the better the idea seemed. Pops would grow corn and tomatoes, lettuce and eggplant, too. He would grow everything in the Burpee catalog. He would be so busy planting and raking and weeding and harvesting that he would hardly have a spare moment to miss her after she was gone.

Clutching the catalog, Lindy went over to the couch and sat down next to Pops. "Why don't you grow some corn this year?" she asked, holding her finger to mark the corn pages.

"Well, I don't know, Lindy. Would you like us to have some corn?"

Lindy nodded. "Look at all the different kinds."

Pops studied the page she showed him. "Might be nice to grow some Silver Beauty. 'Our sweetest corn ever.' Or this one, Pride of Iowa. We're pretty proud, aren't we?"

"You could grow tomatoes, too." She turned to the tomato section, with each tomato bigger and redder than the next, and waited for Pops's reaction.

"Here's one: Tall Boy. 'Plants grow ten feet tall,' it says. I'd have to pick them with a stepladder." Pops held the picture at arm's length. "Ten feet tall," he repeated. "What will they think of next?"

Lindy took the catalog again and looked some more. In another month or so it would be spring.

"In another month I could start spading, if we get a good thaw," Pops said, counting the weeks in his mind. "Be nice to put in some peas, and they get planted early. What do you think? How about some fresh young peas?"

But Lindy was lost in her own thoughts. She had found the absolutely most wonderful page of the catalog. It was a page of miniature vegetables: cherry tomatoes and carrots no bigger than her pinky, doll-sized ears of corn and itsy-bitsy string beans. The photographs showed their true scale, with the cherry tomato perched on top of a thimble, and a perfectly formed ear of corn nestling in the palm of someone's hand. It was the food people would grow in Andorra.

Pops chuckled. "We could get you a little patch of garden, too."

Her own garden! Lindy looked again at the tiny ear of corn and the two-inch carrot. In a few months she would have a miniature basket full of them. That was, of course, if she wasn't already in New York.

Gram came in with Pops's cookies. "It's too bad you missed these when they were warm," she said. "But at least you're up now. How anyone can sleep in the middle of the afternoon I don't know."

"Now, don't be cross, Mother. Lindy and I are planning you a garden."

"As if it hasn't been forty years that I've been saying we should have one."

Lindy looked up, worried. What if Pops was just talking about the garden, and it was never going to happen—like fishing or poker down at the firehouse? But Pops put aside the catalog with a big smile.

"In six weeks I'll be planting peas," he said. "Wait and see."

School was closed on Monday, but by Tuesday the snowplows were able to make it through to clear the road. After the plows had passed, the drifts on either side were as high as Pops's waist. It had been the third big snow of the winter, leaving three layers of hard-packed snow and ice. Lindy wanted them all to melt so that the fields would be bare and brown again.

There was rehearsal every day at school, from two-thirty until three, though the play was still more than a month away. Lindy looked forward to that half hour all day long.

Mrs. Adams knew a lot more about acting than Lindy would have given her credit for. She didn't look at all like an actress, with her hard black bun and ramrod posture, but when she said King Midas's lines she really sounded like a king. Lindy didn't know why Mrs. Adams hadn't left for Broadway years ago.

It was fun having both Nan and Alice in the play, but Lindy sometimes wished they would take their parts more seriously. Alice still didn't know her lines by heart, and Nan still laughed too much at her own funny comments. The worst thing was that neither of them seemed to *believe* in her part. When Lindy rehearsed with them she could tell that they remained Nan and Alice, reciting lines someone else had written. Lindy wanted to *be* Marigold, and how could Princess Marigold talk to Alice Miller and Nan Daniels? If Lindy was going to triumph as an actress, Nan and Alice would have to do their share.

Finally, one day toward the end of February, when the play was only two weeks away, Lindy tried to tell them. They were sitting in the lunchroom, talking about all the terrible things they hoped wouldn't happen during the play. Alice hoped she wouldn't forget her lines, and Lindy hoped her crown wouldn't fall off.

"I hope I don't burst out laughing in the middle of my funny scene," Nan said, unwrapping her peanut butter sandwich.

"The *nurse* shouldn't have to worry about laughing," Lindy said. "She doesn't realize that she's being funny. When she pronounces her words wrong and gets every-thing bungled, she *thinks* she's getting everything right."

"But *I'm* not the nurse."

"But you *are*. You should be."

Nan and Alice exchanged looks.

"And you *are* the queen, Alice. When you gather up the golden flowers, you should have tears in your eyes, real tears. You never sound like you're sad at all."

"Well, thanks a lot," Alice said.

"Do you have any other helpful suggestions?" Nan asked.

"I'm just telling you this so the play will be even better—"

"And you'll be an even bigger star?" Nan finished. "I think you're thinking you're pretty special, Lindy Webster. Well, you're not the only one in the play, and maybe you're not as good as you think you are."

Tears stung Lindy's eyes. They were being so unfair, both of them. She didn't think she was better than they were. No, that wasn't true, either. She did think she was better, but that was only because she *was* better. She had a special talent. She was going to be an actress.

But Nan and Alice looked angry and hurt, and Lindy wished she had never opened her mouth. "Don't be mad, please don't," she said in a small voice. "I'm sorry I talked that way. I didn't mean anything."

Nan and Alice exchanged another look.

"We're not mad," Nan said, and Alice gave a smile. But it wasn't a very big smile.

"So we're still friends?" Lindy asked.

"Of course we are," Nan said. "I mean, of course, Your Royal Highness."

FIFTEEN

The week before the play, one pale purple crocus pushed its way through the melting snow next to the porch steps. That was the first sign of spring. Gram saw a robin redbreast two days later, when she was hanging out a load of wash to dry in the stiff March wind. It was too early to plant anything, but Pops, true to his words, had begun spading. The earth he turned up was rich and dark and moist, good Iowa corn-growing soil. Lindy wondered if her miniature ears would be counted in that fall's grand harvest total.

The plowed drifts by the side of the road shrank every day, and while she waited for the bus in the morning, Lindy kicked off loose chunks to speed the melting along. Tufts of bright green onion grass sprang up everywhere. Lindy nibbled on them as she walked to the carousel after rehearsals. Onion grass was the way spring *tasted*.

The field down by the carousel was soft and muddy, and Lindy left oozing footprints as she crossed back and forth. But inside the old barn nothing had changed. In the old days, she imagined, painters and carpenters had come each spring to refurbish the carousel for a new season. There had been the sound of busy hammering and the smell of fresh paint. Now everything was still and musty from dozens of winters.

Lindy wanted spring to come to the carousel. She wanted to fling open the closed doors and welcome in the wind and sunshine. But the animals would still be so old and tired, so cracked and faded. She wanted to make them young again with the spring. Somehow she would feel better leaving Gram and Pops behind in Three Churches if the carousel came to life again.

Maybe she could do it, all by herself! Lindy jumped off the lion's broad back, enchanted with the thought. She could save her allowance and buy paint at Grove Hardware—shiny, glossy paints in all different colors. The seal would be sleek and black, and his beach ball would be every color of the rainbow. The giraffe would be spotted orange and brown, all the way up his long, long neck.

But his neck would still be so deeply cracked. You couldn't fill a crack like that with paint. Lindy would have to get putty, too, like Pops used to seal the storm windows against the winter. And she remembered from watching Pops paint the house that you couldn't just stick your brush in the can and start painting. First you had to scrape off the old paint, or the new paint would be uneven and lumpy. When Pops painted the house, he rented a special machine from the hardware store, and removing the old paint took him most of two days. Did you *have* to rent the special machine, though? Maybe you could do all the scraping by hand. It would take much longer that way, but after the play Lindy would have lots of time.

She scratched tentatively at one chip of paint on the lion's back. It came off easily, and even though the next chip didn't, Lindy felt elated. She was sure she could do all the work herself.

Scooping up her satchel of books, she hurried from the carousel barn across the fairgrounds and along the road to town. It stayed lighter longer each day now, and the sun lay thick and gold across the sodden fields that would soon be planted with corn. She walked so fast she was practically running, but when she reached Necker Brothers, she stopped to catch her breath. A year ago she could have gone by Pops's small back office to wait for a ride home. But now Pops was home already, watching for her out the front window.

She wished she could tell him about the carousel. Pops knew all there was to know about paint and putty and sanding and scraping. She told Pops everything that happened at school and rehearsal; she told him things she wouldn't have told Gram. Pops understood and appreciated her even if Nan and Alice didn't. But to tell him about the carousel would mean telling him everything, because the carousel was where she went to hide from Three Churches, to plan how she would leave Three Churches behind forever.

The cars that passed her on the Post Road had begun to switch on their headlights. Lindy shouldered her book bag once more and walked slowly and sadly the rest of the way home.

SIXTEEN

From behind a hole in the curtain, Lindy could see the auditorium filling up. Nan's parents were there, in the third row center. Alice's were farther toward the back. Tommy Tillson's mother stood in the aisle, beckoning emphatically to her husband, who had stopped to talk with somebody else's father. The fourth and sixth grades would troop in right before the performance.

In the very first row sat Gram and Pops. They had been the only ones in the auditorium when Lindy first peeked out half an hour ago, waiting proudly for the curtain to go up, all dressed up in their Sunday church clothes. The first row probably wasn't the best place to sit. They would have to crane their necks to see the stage, and at that distance the makeup would look garish and artificial. But Lindy knew that Pops would have sat right up on the stage if he could have. He wasn't going to miss a thing.

"I've invited Mr. Farrington to come see us," Mrs. Adams said, coming up behind Lindy to secure her crown with another bobby pin. Mr. Farrington was the superintendent of schools for the whole county. "I told him to expect something special."

Lindy's eyes widened, and she hurried back to the peephole for another look. She saw the superintendent's bald head and neat bowtie toward the rear of the auditorium. Maybe it would be Mr. Farrington who would explain to Gram and Pops that they had to let her go to New York. She gave her crown a pat. With someone so important in the audience, it had better stay put.

Meg, one of the three ladies-in-waiting, crept over next to Lindy. Beneath her thick powder and rouge, she was grayish white with stage fright.

"I—can't go on," she croaked.

"Sure you can," Lindy said, trying to put Mr. Farrington out of her mind. "You were perfect at the dress rehearsal."

Meg clutched Lindy's arm. "But that was rehearsal. I just know I'll forget my lines. I just know that they'll have to prompt me, and everyone will laugh, and I'll die, Lindy, I'll die!"

"You know your lines inside out," Lindy said. "You're the last person who would forget them."

"Say them with me one more time, okay?"

Lindy nodded, and Meg stuck her small nose high in the air. "'But, my dear, the king isn't half as rich as he pretends to be.'"

Lindy took the part of the second lady-in-waiting. "'Yes, but I've heard tales . . .'" She put her lips to Meg's ear.

"'*Everything* he touches turns to gold!'"

"'To *gold*?!'" Lindy echoed, in the third lady's high voice.

"'To gold,'" she finished, having become the second lady again, while Meg made her eyes wide with astonishment. "There, see? You know them."

Lindy knew all the lines, her own, Meg's, the king's, everyone's. She had been nervous and frightened last time, taking care of props all by herself, but she had no fears about acting. Marigold's part came to her naturally, in a way that remembering other sorts of things never could. Her only problem would be remembering to wait for laughter or applause to die out before going on with her next line. She believed the part so strongly as she acted that it would be hard for her to take account of the audience's reactions. As far as Marigold was concerned, there was no stage or auditorium, just an ancient sunny courtyard, lined with her beloved flowers.

"Two minutes," Mrs. Adams hissed. Lindy smoothed the folds of her long, yellow dress. When the curtain opened, King Midas would be alone onstage, but Marigold would enter next.

Mrs. Adams gave the boys the signal to raise the curtain. Slowly the heavy folds of crimson velvet creaked upward. The audience murmured in appreciation as the palace courtyard came into view, but they became instantly silent when King Midas began to speak.

The king sat counting his store of golden coins, fondling each one lovingly, and telling the audience of his hunger for riches.

"'No, I shall not rest until my treasure has been increased a hundredfold, and then a hundredfold again!'"

That was Lindy's cue, and she danced onstage, ready to cajole the king to come and play with her. But as the bright stage lights temporarily blinded her, she felt her insides suddenly clutch with fear. The lights were so bright that she couldn't see anyone in the audience, but she knew they were there, dozens of people, Gram and Pops and Mr. Farrington, all waiting expectantly for Marigold to utter her first line.

And Lindy had forgotten it.

She didn't even know how to go about trying to remember it. *Pies, pies*—something about pies? No, those lines belonged to a different play altogether. She stood as silent and stricken as the golden statue, frozen in the glare of the spotlight. Tommy, seated before his treasure chest, mouthed something to her, but she could make no sense of his lips. Paralyzed with fear, she couldn't even run offstage to complete her humiliation.

"'Father! Father! Leave aside your coins and come and play with me!'"

Lindy heard a loud whisper offstage, so loud that the whole audience could hear every syllable. The words sounded familiar. "'Father! Father!'" Those were her lines, Marigold's lines. She was Princess Marigold, daughter of miserly King Midas, who loved gold more than life itself, but loved her more than gold. But she didn't feel like Princess Marigold. She felt like Lindy Webster, with a crown of tinfoil-covered cardboard slipping down the back of her head.

"'Father! Father!'" Lindy repeated numbly. Her voice rang strangely in her ears, like a voice heard under water, and she couldn't tell if it was too loud or too soft, if she was shouting or whispering. She forced herself to skip awkwardly across the stage to where Tommy sat on his plywood throne, but her second line came out stiffly as the first: "'Leave aside your coins and come and play with me.'" But Lindy didn't want anyone to play with her; she wanted the play to be over, and then she wanted to crawl away and die.

Lindy never knew how she survived the next half hour. She didn't forget any more lines, but she uttered every one like a sleepwalker mumbling in a dream, and all her gestures felt as jerky as a wooden marionette's. Nan said her funny lines, laughing as she said them, and the audience howled with her; Alice managed to squeeze out one real tear, and the audience sat in sympathetic silence. For Lindy it was all one seamless nightmare.

Offstage before her tantrum scene, she tried one last time to make herself believe that she really *was* a king's daughter who really had discovered her favorite posies turned to lifeless gold. Choking with genuine misery and disappointment, she threw herself on the dusty floor with more feeling than she had managed to summon up during the rest of her performance. At least in that one scene she didn't disgrace herself.

As she froze into statue form, the distant sound of applause rippled at her from far away, but she took no pleasure in it. She was just so relieved to be a statue. At least that part of her role came effortlessly.

Finally, the curtain lumbered down, and the play was over at last. One by one, the cast ran out to take their bows as the audience clapped and stomped its feet. When Nan's turn came, the applause was deafening: the fourth grade boys whistled, and a couple of fathers shouted "Bravo!" Lindy shrank back from her turn, but Mrs. Adams pushed her forward. She gave one quick curtsey and darted back again, only to have to take a second bow with Tommy. The audience kept clapping, but their applause couldn't take away her own keen sense of shame and mortification. She was afraid to look down at Pops. He knew how badly she had failed, even if the fifth-graders didn't know any better.

Back in the fifth-grade room, everyone crowded around Nan to congratulate her. Lindy heard Mr. Farrington's loud deep voice, booming above the others. "Well, I guess you stole the show, young lady," he said, shaking Nan's hand.

Several parents made a point of smiling at Lindy and complimenting her performance, but their polite praise only made her feel worse inside. Across the room she could see Mrs. Adams talking to Gram and Pops. This was to have been the big important conference that would send Lindy off to be a Broadway star and change her life forever. How could she have been so foolish? No wonder Mrs. Adams had never left for Broadway. There was a lot more to acting than convincing performances in front of your grandfather and an eighty-four-year-old dog.

Pops came up to her then, holding out a cup of red punch. "Thirsty, honey?"

Lindy shook her head. For the first time during the whole gruesome afternoon, she felt like crying.

"Everybody's nervous the first time," Pops said. "All those big movie stars, they were all nervous the first time."

"Oh, Pops."

"How about a brownie?" Pops asked, picking up the closest refreshment tray with a conspiratorial grin.

Lindy smiled crookedly and, half-laughing, half-crying, reached for the moistest, chewiest one.

SEVENTEEN

The night before Joan came home for Easter vacation, Lindy had a hard time sleeping. Her new method of making herself fall asleep was a long chain of "God blesses." She would start with Gram and Pops and Joan, and then move on to everyone in the fifth-grade class, and the mailman, and the senior and junior Necker brothers, and . . . She would usually fall asleep somewhere after "God bless Bowker of Bowker Feed." But tonight she had asked God to bless every single person she could think of in Three Churches, and she still lay wide-awake.

Maybe she needed to expand the circle of her blessing a little wider. There were probably thousands of people in New York that Joan could bless by now, hundreds in Aunt Bea's apartment building alone. "God bless Kellogg of Kellogg's Corn Flakes," Lindy prayed under her breath. "God bless Betty Crocker."

Lindy rolled onto her side and pulled the covers up around her nose. She could hardly believe she would see her sister tomorrow, for the first time in almost eight months. Pops would drive to the airport again, as slowly as he had driven the last time, and there Joan would be, home from New York. Gram had been baking for days in preparation for the homecoming, and Pops had been whistling merrily as he worked in the garden. Someone from church had even called a reporter on the *Evening Sentinel*. There would be a big article on Joan in the Sunday edition.

Lindy was bursting with pride and excitement. She hoped she wouldn't feel shy with someone who had become so grand and important. But she couldn't let herself feel shy with Joan. Because there was something she had to tell Joan, and she couldn't tell anyone else.

She had decided to tell Joan that she wanted to go to New York, too. She had tried her best to find some way of leaving on her own and had failed miserably. There was nothing left now but to come right out and ask Joan for help.

Whenever Lindy remembered the play, she cringed. Could she really have thought that Mr. Farrington would rush up to Gram and Pops after the final curtain and make some great proclamation about her talent? Joan had been dancing for nine years, nine whole, long, grueling years, before Aunt Bea issued her invitation. Lindy couldn't think of a single day when Joan hadn't stood at the barre, drenched in sweat, working through her exercises over and over again. Lindy had been in exactly one play, and the play had been exactly one disaster. No one was going to pay her way to Broadway or Hollywood.

She had thought a lot about how to tell her sister that she wanted to go. Maybe Joan would say it first: "Lindy, I've just had the most wonderful idea. Why don't you come back with me? I'm sure Aunt Bea won't mind, and then we'll never have to be apart again." But Joan was obviously getting along very well without Lindy. Come to think of it, Lindy had gotten used to their separation, too. She didn't really miss her sister anymore, not the way she had in the beginning. She just needed to get away.

What if Joan didn't want her to come? Joan might feel that Aunt Bea had already been generous enough to one sister—it wasn't fair to expect her to take in another. Or Joan might want New York to stay her own private world. Lindy understood needing a special, secret place. She still had not told anyone about the carousel.

If Joan didn't invite her, Lindy wouldn't ask to go. Even after her humiliation in the play, Lindy had some pride left. But she would have to make sure Joan knew how much she wanted the invitation. It would be terrible if years later Joan were to say, "But, Lindy, I thought all along that you loved Three Churches!"

Of course, she *did* love Three Churches. And she loved Gram and Pops. She turned over on her other side, too sleepy now to think clearly.

"God bless Duncan Hines," she murmured, and fell asleep, dreaming that her mother and father were bending over her bed, blessing her as she slept.

"So those fancy New York City folks liked your dancing, did they?" Pops asked, laying another savory slice of ham on Joan's plate.

"Well, I'm just in the corps de ballet, so I'm not sure they liked me more than anybody else," Joan said matter-of-factly.

"The corps de ballet! Did you hear that, Mother?"

"That's very nice," Gram said. "Now, have some more biscuits, Joan. I'm not letting you go back until you look less like a starved cat."

"Oh, Gram," Joan said. "Dancers have to be skinny."

Unmoved, Gram held out the basket of biscuits. Joan took her third.

"Tell me everything about Three Churches," Joan said when she had done her duty by the first half of the biscuit. "That's what I want to hear."

"Nothing much to tell," Pops said. "We had some record snow here back in February, so we were laid up pretty good for a while. Planted my peas on time, though, all the same."

"Old Miss Anderson from church passed away last month," Gram said.

Joan made a sympathetic little noise.

"Sometimes these things are for the best," Gram said.

"Well, now, you're pretty quiet, Lindy," Pops said. "You must have a lot to tell your sister."

Lindy spooned more raisin sauce onto her last bite of ham. She wanted to tell Joan about the little countries project and her new miniature garden, but she couldn't let Joan think she was happy and content in Three Churches, or the plan wouldn't work.

"It must be exciting to live in New York," she said. That was a good opening.

"I guess so. There's something happening every day."

"Do you ride on the subway?" Joan had written about the subway in her letters, but Lindy wasn't quite sure what else to ask.

"You know I do. It's really, really dirty, though, and pretty dangerous. I'd never ride it late at night."

Lindy had been hoping Joan would speak about the subway a little more enthusiastically. But she went ahead with her next line, anyway. "I've never seen a subway." She took another bite of ham. "I'd like to see one, though, I really would." Now was the time for Joan to invite her to come, at least for a visit.

"They're not much to see," Joan said.

Lindy tried again. "Have you been to the top of the Empire State Building?"

"Not yet. It's very expensive, and half the time you can't see anything with all the pollution. Mostly just the tourists go." Joan wasn't a tourist. She was a real New Yorker.

"I wouldn't trust an elevator to take me all the way to the top of one of those skyscrapers," Gram said. "If the cable snaps, that's the end."

"I'm sure they're safe," Joan said. "I hope so. Aunt Bea lives on the twenty-seventh floor."

Lindy could hardly imagine living that high up in a building. She wasn't sure she'd like it. Now in the spring she could look out her window and see the cherry tree all in bloom. Up twenty-seven stories it would be practically like living in outer space. But then she remembered the point of all her questions.

"Oh, Joan," she said. "It must be beautiful."

"You get used to it," Joan said. "Unless there's a blackout, and you have to walk up twenty-seven flights."

"Is there a spectacular view?"

"Not really. Just a bunch of other apartment buildings."

"How big is Aunt Bea's apartment?" Lindy asked casually. She was almost ready to give up.

"It's pretty small."

"But not *too* small." Surely it wasn't too small to fit another person.

"Well, it's small," Joan said. She pointed to her empty plate. "See, Gram, I finished the biscuit. But now I couldn't eat another bite."

"Nonsense," Gram said. "Help me clear the table, will you, Lindy? There's pie for dessert."

When Lindy and Joan were alone in their room Easter night, Lindy gave one more try.

"I miss you," she said as Joan bent her forehead flat against her outstretched leg. "I wish you didn't have to go away again."

"Me, too," Joan said. "I mean, I'm glad I'm going, I need to go, it's the only way I'm ever going to be a dancer. But I wish I could come home more often."

Lindy remembered Christmas with a pang of bitterness. But it was Joan who had missed all the fun. There had been none of Gram's gingerbread cookies in New York, and no pinkish white king for Aunt Bea's manger, and no lovingly carved wooden dolls. It had served Joan right for disappointing Gram and Pops that way.

"Maybe I could visit you sometime," Lindy said lightly, waiting for Joan's face to light up with pleasure.

"Maybe sometime."

"I could come for the summer. There's only two months left of school, and I could come right away when school ended and stay until September." She had promised herself not to ask, but nothing was going as she had planned.

Joan stopped stretching. "But Gram and Pops would miss you so much."

The unfairness of Joan's words struck Lindy like a sharp slap. "But *you* left. *You* went away and never even came back for Thanksgiving or Christmas. They wait every day for the mail, and half the time you don't even write—"

"I *know*, Lindy. I don't need you to remind me about it."

"So why can't I come, too?"

Joan didn't say anything for a minute. "It's not the same," she said finally. "It just isn't. I've waited all my life for something like this to happen to me. I have to be a dancer, don't you see? Mother always wanted me to be a dancer. . . ." Joan spread her hands helplessly, waiting for Lindy to interrupt her, to tell her that she understood.

But Lindy wouldn't. "What about me?" she asked in a hard, shrill voice. She hated herself for whining, but she couldn't help it anymore. "Don't you ever think about anyone but yourself? Don't you think I want things, too?"

"And going to New York, that's what you want?"

"Yes!"

Joan got up from the bed and walked slowly over to Lindy's bureau. She picked up one of Lindy's small pink barrettes and snapped it open and shut again with ferocious concentration.

"Okay," she said, whirling around. "If you want to come, I'll ask Aunt Bea. But just do me one favor, think about it for a while, will you?"

"I've been thinking about it all year," Lindy said.

"Okay," Joan said. "I'll ask her. Okay? Are you satisfied?"

"Yes," Lindy said. "I'm satisfied." Her heart swelled to bursting. She rolled away from Joan and stared at the wall next to her small white bed. Pops had hung that apple blossom wallpaper almost seven years ago, when she and Joan had first come to Three Churches. Now, if Aunt Bea said it was all right, Lindy would be leaving Three Churches forever.

Lindy knew that Aunt Bea would let her come, and Gram and Pops would say good-bye to her as they had said good-bye to Joan. Lindy would ride the subway and live in a skyscraper and see the ocean and never wait for the mail again.

Like King Midas, Lindy would get the wish she wanted. And yet the apple blossoms grew blurry as Lindy looked at them through eyes filled with tears.

EIGHTEEN

In the weeks following Joan's visit, Lindy looked every day for a letter from New York saying that things were settled, but the letter didn't come. Lindy knew that Joan was giving her time to change her mind, time to admit that she didn't really mean what she had said, that she didn't really want to go. But Joan should have known Lindy was too stubborn for that.

As each day went by without a letter, though, it was harder and harder to believe that she would truly be leaving. The fields had been plowed and planted for the next harvest of corn, and small white butterflies fluttered again in the tall grass by the side of the road. The flowering dogwood tree in front of the house snowed fragrant white petals on the young lawn, and the cherry tree outside Lindy's window was decked out like a rosy bride.

Even Shep was crazy with the splendor of spring. He tore in dizzy circles around Gram's bed of red and yellow tulips for all the world as if he were a puppy, instead of a stately, dignified old dog. It occurred to Lindy that when she went away she might never see Shep again. On his next birthday he would be thirteen, and for a dog that was the same as being ninety-one. So Lindy spent long hours talking to him as he half-dozed in the warm spring sun.

Pops's peas were knee-high, and he had to stretch twine between two stakes for them to cling to as they grew. They would be ripe in June, and Gram had promised Lindy that she could shell the first supper's panful. In her own small garden, the first sprouts of miniature corn and tomatoes had pushed themselves up through the soil, a narrow line of pale green shoots. Lindy hovered over them with an anxious, motherly eye, worried that the heavy April rain would drive them back into the ground. But they kept on growing through sun and shower, and Shep frightened away any rabbits that might have fancied them for a light lunch.

Lindy walked to the carousel almost every day. On each visit she did more scraping and sanding, borrowing sandpaper sheet by sheet from Pops's basement workbench. She had almost finished removing all the old paint from the giraffe—the wood underneath was sleek and smooth after she sanded it. She couldn't bear to think she might have to leave before she ever got to painting.

In another two weeks, her Nations of the World project was due at school. Pops had suggested sending away for information to the United Nations in New York and the State Department in Washington, D.C., and bulging envelopes had come back filled with maps and facts and colored pictures. Her project would be the best in the class by far. The only thing that made her sad was that her pen pal had never written back. Lindy had been so excited to finally get a pen pal from Andorra, and she had written to her twice. Maybe it took extra long for the mail to find a country so small.

The final play of the year was scheduled for the middle of June. Lindy wasn't going to mention it at home, but Pops asked her if there were going to be any more plays, and she didn't like to tell outright lies.

"It's *Hansel and Gretel*," she said, kneeling next to Pops out in the garden as he weeded his peas for the dozenth time.

"Which part do you want?"

"Oh, I just want to be props again." She looked down intently at a fat worm poking his head up where Pops had weeded.

"Now, why's that, honey? It seems a shame to waste a talent like yours—"

"I don't have any talent."

Pops put down his trowel and wiped his hands on his handkerchief. "Of course you do. I don't know when anyone's made me laugh like you did with those pies."

"But that was just at home with you and Shep. When it was the real play I was the worst in the whole class." The worm stretched itself luxuriously in the sunlight and wriggled back into the earth again.

"Look at me, honey." Lindy reluctantly met Pops's eyes. "Rome wasn't built in a day. You have to keep on trying and trying and when you've tried as hard as you can, you try some more. You won't be as nervous the next time."

"How do you know?"

"Promise me that you'll give it a try, honey, that's all. It can't hurt just to try."

Lindy had a fleeting glimpse of herself as the wicked witch, shrieking horribly at a horrified Hansel and Gretel from the roof of her gingerbread house.

"Okay," she said. "I'll try."

At long last, Gram's log cabin quilt was almost finished. All the thousands of tiny colored strips had been pieced together, and the dark strips and light strips undulated hypnotically in one great ocean of color. Pops set up Gram's quilting frame in the middle of the living room, and Gram sat day after day taking the perfectly uniform, almost invisibly small stitches that would bind the layers of piecing, batting, and backing into one finished quilt.

Lindy had helped with the piecing throughout the long fall and winter, but Gram was doing the quilting herself. Every stitch showed, and she couldn't count on Lindy's stitches to be small and even enough. So Lindy just stood and watched.

"Can you tell which strips I pieced?" Lindy asked. They all looked the same to her.

"I think some of yours are in this corner I'm working on now," Gram said. Lindy studied them. They did look a little more crooked than the others.

"I wish you knew for sure. Then if I ever went away, every time you looked at those strips you'd remember how I sewed them for you."

"You sewed a lot of them, I remember that, sitting there with your long, glum face, as bored as could be."

"I wasn't really bored," Lindy said. Gram looked over at her skeptically. "I was just—kind of bored."

Lindy traced the perfectly straight line of Gram's quilting stitches with her index finger. "Don't you ever get bored, Gram? After you've sewed fifty thousand strips, doesn't the next one start to get boring?"

"No," Gram said, "I can't say it does. The way I see it, Lindy, is that most folks get about as bored as they want to. There's always something about the world that's interesting, if you've eyes to see it. Even after fifty thousand strips, there's always one that's different, if you want there to be. I think that's why I keep on quilting."

Gram rethreaded her needle, but she didn't start sewing right away. "It's because it's so much like life. You're given what you're given to work with, fabric from clothes your children and grandchildren have outgrown, some extra bolts you picked up at a yard sale. Like, that there's your Sunday best from two summers ago, that little blue floral print. And I got that green at the church rummage sale a year ago this spring.

"But you take what you're given and you put it together any way you like. Nobody told me to put that blue and green next to each other like that. It was up to me to stitch it all together as I saw best. And if I don't like how I stitched it, I guess it's no one's fault but mine. But it's likely I'm boring you now with all this chattering."

"You're not boring me," Lindy said. She watched Gram sew until her needle ran out of thread again, and then Lindy stepped out onto the front porch, as pink and purple feathers by the pillowful were emptied into the sunset sky. A breeze had started up, and the wispy feather-clouds drifted back and forth just above the horizon.

So it was up to Lindy to decide what kind of quilt she wanted to make out of her life, that was what Gram was saying. When Joan first went away, Lindy had seen her life as a drab, faded quilt, like the dark gray Amish one Gram and Pops had on their bed upstairs. Gram always marveled over the exquisite quilting, but all Lindy could see was its vast, unrelieved grayness. And that was how her life had looked, too.

But then Lindy had found out that she had her own special talent. Acting was like a bright yellow square stitched into that great expanse of gray. And even though it wasn't as big or bright as she had tried to think it was, the quilt had many bright patches now. She and Pops worked in their gardens side by side, and the daffodils were in full bloom, and Gram had made bread pudding specially for Lindy just the night before. And there was the carousel, with the giraffe almost ready for a fresh new coat of orange and brown spots. Even the gray background didn't seem drab or faded anymore.

And all that had really changed was the way Lindy looked at it. Just like Gram and the fifty-thousandth strip, Lindy could choose to look at her life however she wanted to.

"Better come in for a sweater, child, if you're going to stay out there in the damp," Gram called through the open window.

"I'm coming in," Lindy said. It didn't matter how she looked at things, anyway, if she was going to leave them all behind her and never look back.

NINETEEN

Every spring as the first green and red buds appeared on the bare tree branches, Pops promised Joan and Lindy that all the leaves would be out by May 15th. He gave the date with such precision and certainty that Lindy pictured the very last little leaf scrambling frantically to open up by 11:59 P.M. on the 14th.

It was May 16th now, and if there was a leaf that hadn't opened Lindy couldn't find it. Everywhere was green, and once again there was shade—cool, dark pools underneath the trees.

Lindy had spent the morning at the carousel, cackling hoarsely in preparation for *Hansel and Gretel*. As the witch she was going to have a long green nose and a stringy black wig. Even the carousel animals would tremble to see her in full costume. Lindy hadn't known if Mrs. Adams would trust her again with such a major role after *The Golden Touch,* but no one else seemed to think Lindy's performance had been as terrible as she remembered it. In any case, she was the witch now, and she wasn't going to let herself be paralyzed with fear ever again. Hansel and Gretel could be afraid, but not the witch in all her splendid wickedness.

When she reached home after her long walk, Gram and Pops were off on their Saturday errands. Lindy poured herself a glass of Gram's homemade lemonade, first of the season, and grabbed a handful of oatmeal raisin cookies from Gram's great earthenware jar. With lemonade in one hand and cookies in the other, she strolled into the living room to see if there was any mail.

Pops had left the mail on the walnut table by the front window, and Lindy could hardly believe her eyes when she saw what lay on the top of the pile. A thin, airmail letter with a bright foreign stamp was addressed to:

> *Linda Webster*
> *191 North Post Road*
> *Three Churches*
> *Iowa*
> *United States of America*
> *North America*
> *Earth*
> *Solar System*
> *Milky Way Galaxy*
> *Universe*
> *Mind of God*

It was the way Lindy had given her return address on her second letter to her pen pal in Andorra! Her fingers trembling, she slit open the envelope with Pops's brass letter opener. It was hard to make out her pen pal's handwriting, with its cramped, foreign style, and Catalina had certain problems writing in English, but Lindy pored over every word. As far as she could make out, Catalina couldn't get over what long addresses Americans had; she had two brothers and one sister, but no pets; she liked school, except for spelling and arithmetic; she, too, lived in a small village where nothing ever happened and everything was the same every day.

Lindy folded the letter reverently after she had read it four times. She felt the same way about the letter that she felt about the Scandinavian straw ornaments on the Christmas tree. They had come so many thousands of miles to somehow find their way to Three Churches, Iowa, one tiny, insignificant corner of the universe and the mind of God, but—she was coming more and more to realize— the corner Lindy loved best.

Hugging the letter to her, Lindy almost didn't notice the second letter in the pile, but as she was about to turn and run upstairs it suddenly caught her eye. It was addressed to her, too, and, staring at it, Lindy felt overcome with a heavy, cold sadness. The letter was from Joan.

Lindy picked it up slowly. As she reached for Pops's letter opener again, she saw that it had already been opened. Pops must not have noticed the address—it was the first letter Joan had written just to Lindy since last summer's letters from ballet camp. Horrified, Lindy tore the letter from the envelope and frantically scanned Joan's few lines:

Dear Lindy,
   I finally talked to Aunt Bea. She says you're

welcome to come live here, and she'll write to
Gram and Pops in a couple of days. I wanted you to
get this first just in case you've changed your mind
and this isn't what you want anymore. But if you
still want to come, it's fine with me. Really.

> *Love,*
> *Joan*

Lindy didn't wait to put the letter back on the pile. Letting it flutter to the floor, she bolted out the front door and flew down to the Post Road, as if she were running for her life.

Lindy hadn't known she could run so fast and so far. But she had to get away before Gram and Pops got home. She could never face them again, that much was certain. How Pops must have felt when he opened that letter! He had probably been so pleased to see it, too, anticipating breezy, cheerful news from Joan, maybe word that she was coming home for her summer vacation. Instead he found out that behind his back Lindy, too, had been making plans to leave him.

She sped through the center of town and out the South Post Road, crouching down in the tall grass or ducking into doorways in case Gram and Pops should drive by. Thank goodness she had never told anyone about her secret carousel! Not that Pops and Gram would even come to look for her. They would be relieved that she was gone, now that they knew how selfish and ungrateful she had been. But Shep would miss her—Shep could forgive her anything.

The most terrible thing was that now Lindy had no choice but to go to New York. She could never go back to Gram and Pops, never again sleep in her little bed under the eaves by the flowering cherry tree. Her miniature garden on which she had lavished so much love would be choked with giant weeds. The corn would be all in tassel—Pops's corn that she had helped him plant—and Lindy would be far away where there were no trees or flowers or anything.

She remembered that she had no food or clothing, no blanket to soften the carousel's hard floor. But the old fairgrounds outside the carousel were thick with wild flowers. She could sleep outside if it didn't rain. She would have to go looking for edible roots and berries, too, and figure out how to make a fire by rubbing two sticks together. It was still cold in the evenings.

And she had no money at all, not even a dime to call Joan, though sometimes you could find a dime left behind in a phone booth. Maybe she would have to walk all the way to New York, hundreds and hundreds of miles, all by herself. Maybe she would have to go begging. Panting as she ran up to the carousel barn, she flung herself against the creaking old door. Gasping for breath, she managed to pull herself up onto the giraffe's bare, blond back and hunched there in exhausted misery.

Lindy didn't how how many hours she had been sitting there when she heard footsteps, close and growing closer. In all the time she had come to the carousel, she had never seen another living soul. Maybe the carousel belonged to someone, after all, and he would arrest her for trespassing and drag her off to jail. Maybe it was another outlaw, with a long knife and a sinister laugh, who would take her with him as his companion in crime. If he didn't cut her throat instead.

Lindy froze, as still as Marigold's statue, trying to blend in the half-shadow against the giraffe's long neck.

"Lindy?"

It was Pops. The old door creaked as he pushed it open and peered into the carousel barn. "Lindy, are you there?"

How could he possibly have found her? He hadn't seen her yet, though, and she didn't move a muscle, trying with all her might to make herself invisible.

"Honey?"

The pet name made her feel like crying. But she didn't say a word. Pops took one last look around the barn and turned to walk away.

"Wait, Pops! Wait!"

Lindy slid off the giraffe, gulping back a sob. Pops turned around and smiled at her. For a moment they just stood and looked at each other.

"How did you find me?" Lindy asked finally.

"I had a hunch you'd be here, that's all."

"Here?"

"Well, I knew you had some place you must be going to on days when the school bus came home without you. When I was a boy, it was my tree house, twenty feet high in a big old catalpa tree four miles away from home. Thought for sure my dad would never find me there."

"And did he?"

Pops chuckled. "Sure did. I don't reckon I had him fooled a minute and a half."

"But how did you know I was *here*? I never told anyone. No one knows about the carousel but me."

Pops walked slowly over to the carousel and laid his hand on the camel's hump. "I carved this carousel, honey. Fifty years ago this summer."

"You *carved* it?" If Pops had built the Eiffel Tower in Paris, Lindy wouldn't have been more astonished and amazed.

"This carousel was made by G. A. Dentzel, in Philadelphia, and there's never been a finer maker of carousels, let me tell you. I worked in Dentzel's shop for five years, as a carver." Pops looked closely at the camel's proud face. "Yessir, that's my work, Lindy."

Lindy stroked the camel's nose tenderly. *Pops* had carved those drooping eyes, those funny flat ears. Her very own Pops.

"Why did you stop?" If she could make carousels, she would never leave that for anything else.

"Well, come the Depression the business went bust. Those were hard times, you know, and folks had other things to spend their money on. This here's the last carousel I ever worked on."

"So what happened then?" Lindy asked, enchanted.

"Carousels were all I knew, so I got me a job with a touring company that took carousels all around the country, from fair to fair. And by the time *that* went bust, I was lucky enough to have met your grandmother, so I signed on with Necker Brothers right here in Three Churches. I had seen enough of the world by then to have a pretty good idea of where two people could be happy."

"But the carousel?"

"When the company went broke, they sold what they could. What they couldn't sell we had to leave behind, just abandon in some farmer's field. It kind of tore me up to say good-bye to this carousel, though, so I took it apart myself and moved it into this old barn, just to give it a little protection from our Iowa winters. And then I didn't look back. It made me too sad to think of it here, abandoned.

"No, the years haven't been too kind to this carousel, have they?" Pops walked around the carousel, frowning. But when he reached the giraffe, he stopped in surprise. "But someone's been doing some good work here." He looked over at Lindy, and she blushed.

"Do you think it could ever be painted to look the way it was before?" Lindy asked.

"Sure it could. Might not be a bad project for some retired gent with a little know-how." He winked at Lindy, and she threw her arms around the giraffe's long neck.

"Oh, do you think you could?"

"I don't see why not."

He was smiling broadly, but then his expression changed. Lindy remembered why she had come to the carousel, and she looked hard at the camel so she wouldn't have to look at Pops.

"Lindy, listen to me. If you wanted to go to New York with your sister, all you had to do was ask. You know that."

"But I—"

"We know it can't be too easy for you, living here with a couple of old fogies like your grandmother and me."

"You're not old fogies," Lindy said.

"Since your Aunt Bea is willing to take you, we'll pay for your schooling and your board. We've already talked it over, your grandmother and me. Joan loves it in the city, though how she can stand it I'm sure I don't know. Maybe you'd be happier there, too."

"I don't want to go to New York," Lindy said. "I never wanted to go, not really. I want to stay in Three Churches with you and Gram."

"You don't have to say that, honey," Pops said.

"But it's true," Lindy said. And it really was true.

"I could have the carousel running in a couple of months, maybe, if I had the right assistant." Pops held out his hand.

Lindy took it joyfully, and then threw her arms around the giraffe and Pops together. She could hardly wait for summer.

ABOUT THE AUTHOR

CLAUDIA MILLS is the author of *Boardwalk With Hotel,* which is available from Bantam-Skylark Books. Ms. Mills is currently editor at the Center for Philosophy and Public Policy at the University of Maryland. She lives with her husband in Takoma Park, Maryland.

BANTAM SKYLARK BOOKS

A Reading Adventure

A stranger on earth needs Erik's help!

☐ **15438   THE FALLEN SPACEMAN Lee Harding $2.25**
Up above the earth a mysterious spaceship watches.
One small alien, tucked inside a huge spacesuit is
working outside the craft when it suddenly blasts off.
Poor Tyro, alone and frightened is trapped on Earth.
Luckily, it's Erik who finds him first.

Can there be such a thing as too much chocolate?

☐ **15479   THE CHOCOLATE TOUCH Patrick Skene Catling $2.50**
John Midas loves chocolate more than anything else in
the world. Until the day he finds a funny old coin, trades
it for a box of chocolate and—*the chocolate touch.*
Suddenly, everything tastes like chocolate and John finds
out it's possible to get too much of a very good thing.

A family of mice move into Miss Know It All's Good Day Home for Girls

☐ **15373   THE GOOD DAY MICE Carol Beach York $2.25**
Inquisitive Frederick Mouse has been mouse-napped
and the Mouse Family takes up residence in the Good
Day Home For Girls while they search for their missing
son. While Father Mouse investigates, Mother Mouse,
Violet and Baby Mouse wreak havoc beneath the noses
of Mr. Not So Much, Miss Lavender and Miss Plum, and
Tatty, too.

Simon's new best friend is a ghost.

☐ **15486   GHOST IN MY SOUP Judi Miller $2.25**
Something funny is going on at Scott's house.
Someone—or something—is moving things around,
stealing and making all kinds of trouble which Scott
gets blamed for. Only Scott knows what's *really*
going on, and who—or what—is to blame!

The greatest 4-footed detective
of them all in two howling good mysteries

☐ **15260 SEBASTIAN (SUPER SLEUTH) AND THE HAIR OF THE DOG MYSTERY Mary Blount Christian $2.25**

Detective John Quincy Jones *isn't* the best detective ever, but luckily, his sheepdog Sebastian *is*. When the police chief's cat is snatched and an emerald necklace grabbed, Sebastian Super Sleuth leaps into action. And not even an evil gypsy curse can keep this dog-tective from finding the crooks.

☐ **15293 SEBASTIAN (SUPER SLEUTH) AND THE CRUMMY YUMMIES CAPER Mary Blount Christian $2.25**

Chummy the Wonder Dog is missing, stolen from the All-Breed Dog Show. Sebastian, the master of doggie-disguise is hot on the trail, masquerading as an ordinary dog. Dog-nappers beware!

**Join the SKYLARK adventure—
order these books
now!**

Prices and availability subject to change without notice.

☐ **THE OWLSTONE**   15349/$2.50
  CROWN
  by X. J. Kennedy
  When Timothy and Verity Tibbs follow a tiny ladybug
  private eye over a moon-lit path to Other Earth, magical
  adventures happen fast.

☐ **BONES ON BLACK**   15443/$2.25
  SPRUCE MOUNTAIN
  by David Budbill
  Thirteen-year-olds Danny and Seth set out to explore Black
  Spruce Mountain because they love camping out. But
  Black Spruce Mountain appears to be haunted and their
  adventure is more than they bargained for.

☐ **SNOWSHOE TREK TO**   15469/$2.25
  OTTER RIVER
  by David Budbill
  David and Seth have a lot in common besides their age.
  They share a love of adventure and specifically, they share
  a love of camping and exploring. And what better place to
  explore than the backwoods of Vermont?

☐ **CHRISTOPHER**   15363/$2.25
  by Richard M. Koff
  On a dare from a friend, Christopher knocks on the door
  of a haunted house. There he meets the "Headmaster"
  who teaches him how to release the amazing powers of
  his own mind.